a dirty bitches novel

HOT
mess

k.a. ware

Editing by D.E. Howden and R.R. Carlos
Cover Design by Pink Ink Designs
www.pinkinkdesigns.com

Dedication

For my mom.
Thank you for teaching me not to take life too
seriously.

HEATHER-

DON'T BE AFRAID TO
LET YOUR INNER
DIRTY BITCH OUT TO
PLAY!.

Love,
KAREN

Prologue

This is a story full of fuck ups and hilarious hijinks. There is foul language and gratuitous sex, there is heartbreak and love. There are embarrassing moments and ridiculous situations.

***

My name is Briar Jameson and I have the best friends on the planet. Even though they are slightly psychotic and incredibly inappropriate, they are mine. My people.

They say the friends you make when you're young will fade away as you grow older and find yourself. That may be true for some, but not for us. We were lucky.

This is our story, the complicated, the lewd, the heartwarming and the utter insanity of life rolled into one hot mess.

One

I'm Classy Like That

The sound of a chainsaw woke me from a dead sleep.

Cracking an eye open I assessed my surroundings, the first thing my blurry eyes focused on was an Iron Maiden poster.

What the fuck?

The memories from the night before started to flood my mind. It was like when you were a kid and you clicked through your Viewmaster as fast as you could, not caring that there was no way you could fully process each slide, just wanting to see how fast you could go through the pictures. The night started to come together in my mind as I laid there completely still, staring at the poster and listening to the chainsaw beside me, which I now realized was snoring.

Evie had set me up on a blind date with a client from work, the woman was the worst kind of hopeless romantic. She was convinced that everyone else was just as obsessed with finding the *one* as she was. I started to catalog the things I knew for certain; we met at Murphy's, there was a band, we came back to his place... I groaned when I remembered I'd been drinking whiskey, nothing good ever happened when I drank the amber nectar of the Gods. That would at least explain the headache that was splitting my brain in two.

Steeling my nerves, I slowly rolled onto my back and risked a glance at Danny? Davy? No wait, Donny? Fuck! I squeezed my eyes shut and tried to remember his name.

Who forgets the name of the person they slept with the night before? I knew it ended with a 'y'. Mikey, Nicky, Timmy...

"Tommy!" I practically shouted when I remembered his name and immediately cringed, holding as still as humanly possible hoping he wouldn't wake up at my outburst. I didn't even think I was breathing. The loud chainsaw snoring stopped abruptly and a sound that could only be described as someone swallowing their own face followed.

I jerked my head to where Tommy was, and studied his face. More than anything in the world I wanted to sneak out of there without waking him up, but if he was going to choke to death I needed to nut up and risk the awkward morning after. I mean, I'd have to, there was a bar full of people from last night that could testify that we'd left together. I did not need to be the last person that saw him alive. Oh, God, and my DNA was all over his sheets.

Should I wash them?

I wasn't capable of being a murder suspect, they wouldn't even have to strong arm a confession out of me. One look from a detective and I'd crumple like a hungry swimsuit model in a bakery. I was too pretty for prison; I'd seen *Orange is the New Black.* Before the end of my first week in lock up I'd either be dead, or Big Bertha's main bitch.

I chanced another look at Tommy. After my initial freak-out, his snoring seemed to have returned to a safe WeedWacker hum and he was no longer gasping for air.

Thank Christ.

As I started to slide off the bed, I noticed his sheets were black satin, eww. I took in the room as I stood from the bed and almost laughed out loud. This guy's bedroom was like an 80s porno. Black laminate furniture with gold trim and mirrored accents, there were even mirrors on the ceiling.

How did I not notice that before?

A glance at the clock on the nightstand confirmed I had an hour before I needed to be at work. I quickly shimmied into my jeans, and threw on my shirt from last night. Standing in the middle of the room I frantically searched for my bra, only to find it hooked around the largest bong I'd ever seen in my life. It was monstrous, at least three feet tall. I shook my head, this guy just kept getting better and better. Scooping up my bra I shoved it into my purse and made a beeline for the door, shoes in hand.

The sun blinded me as I stepped out the front door and headed down the stairs from his third-floor apartment, stopping at the bottom of the concrete steps to slip on my heels. The parking lot was huge. Glancing from side to side I tried desperately to remember where I'd parked my car.

Shit, what if I left it at the bar?

No, I distinctly remembered following his Kia from the bar. I'd had to walk forever to get to his apartment from the guest parking. I headed towards the club house hoping that was where I'd parked. How did I not see the warning signs with this guy? Either my standards had lowered significantly without my knowledge, or my douchebag radar was seriously in need of calibration. The guy made me park in guest parking out in butt fucking nowhere instead of doing the gentlemanly thing and giving me his reserved spot. Just because you know you're getting laid doesn't mean you get to stop trying, asshat.

I pushed the unlock button on my key fob over and over as I continued my search, finally spotting my car in the distance. It was like an oasis in the desert, except instead of water it held clean underwear. I popped the trunk when I reached the car and sifted through the clothes and shoes in the back.

As a rule, I always kept a few changes of clothes, shoes, clean underwear, and a small emergency makeup bag in my car. You never knew when you were going to need it. Not that I found myself in a predicament where I required such an arsenal often, but a girl should always be prepared.

The time on my phone read 7:45. Shit! I grabbed a pair of slacks and a sweater from the trunk and jumped in the car throwing everything in the passenger seat. When I pulled out on the main road, I recognized where I was, thank fuck for that. After a quick stop at McDonalds, because I was classy like that, I'd changed, my hair was tamed, my makeup had been upgraded from drowned raccoon to work appropriate smoky eye and I was on the road again.

***

"Knees to chest, motherfucker!" I yelled at the lanky man sauntering across the street and directly in the path of where I needed to turn.

My leg was bouncing up and down at a steady rhythm and my fingers were tapping impatiently on the steering wheel in time with my blinker as Captain Stoner continued at a snail's pace. Shaggy brown hair bounced beneath a knit cap with each exaggerated stride. His tie-dyed shirt hung limply off of his skinny shoulders, and I nearly gagged when I noticed the shoes he was wearing as he approached. They were toe shoes, the ones with the rubber soles that molded to the wearers' feet and separated each of their toes. They were the worst thing that had happened to fashion since the invention of Crocs. I shuddered and wiggled my own toes in my pumps in an effort to rid myself of the creepy feeling. I had no idea how anyone could wear those things, I couldn't even stomach toe socks, blah!

"Come on, come on!" I growled through gritted teeth as I slowly inched forward into the intersection. Finally, the man cleared the crosswalk and I was able to turn onto the street that would take me the rest of the way to work. I shot a glance at the clock on my dashboard 8:34. I was already late and I had at least another five-minute drive before I got to the office. It was the third time this week that I'd been late.

I am so going to get written up for this!

I came barreling into the parking lot like I was on the set of *The Dukes of Hazard*, and was surprised my tires didn't screech as I whipped into the parking space. My bag got caught on the emergency brake as I tried to jump out of my car, jerking me back and forcing my head to collide with the doorframe. I cursed under my breath and freed my purse before slamming my car door and running into the building.

Falling into the chair behind my desk I glanced at the clock 8:41. I was panting like I'd run a marathon since I hadn't had time to wait for the elevator and was forced to climb three flights of stairs.

"You're late," Mrs. Callahan said from behind me, causing me to jump.

"I know, I'm sorry—" I began, as I searched my brain for a decent excuse for my tardiness that didn't involve getting drunk last night and waking up in a stranger's apartment.

"This is the third time this week. I'm sorry but I can't have my assistant showing up whenever she feels like it." She didn't sound sorry at all as she glared down her nose at me. Her crisp pant suit and perfectly coifed hair a glaring reminder that she was the complete antithesis to my unorganized and often rumpled self.

"I understand. I promise it won't happen again."

"I know it won't," She said, and I sighed in relief that I'd dodged a bullet. My relief was short lived when she continued, "Because your services will no longer be required. Ms. Jameson, you're fired. You have fifteen minutes to clear your things from your desk and vacate the premises."

I stared in shock as she turned on her heels and walked into her office as if she didn't just turn my entire world upside down. I was not an idiot, I knew it was my fault for being chronically late, but the woman had no fucking heart. People say men are hard asses in the workplace but those people had never worked for Marian Callahan. She was a stone-cold bitch that expected nothing short of perfection. With any luck my next boss wouldn't make me want to day drink as much.

Two

Walk of Shame

There was nothing more humiliating than packing up your desk and doing the I-just-got-canned walk of shame in front of your coworkers. Well, ex-coworkers. The heat emanating from my cheeks could fry an egg. Both anger and shame colored my face as I made my way back out to my car.

I needed to get the fuck out of there, I felt like I was in a goddamn fishbowl. At least three of my former colleagues were standing at the window watching my exit as if my shame was for their personal enjoyment. In a display of the highest level of professionalism, I flipped them off. Not my proudest moment, but come on, they looked like they were about to start tapping on the fucking glass.

After tossing all my shit in the passenger seat, I cranked the engine and threw it in drive, or at least I tried to. The shifter wouldn't move out of park.

Oh, fuck, no, no, no!

I tried again. Nothing. The thing wouldn't budge. My head fell forward in defeat, the worst day ever just kept getting worse. The same thing had happened a few months ago and I tried to remember through the haze of my hangover what my brother had told me to do in this situation. I tried the horn. Nothing. Not even a squeak. I popped the hood, and jumped out of the car.

The peanut gallery must be loving this.

Thank God my brother had the forethought to actually teach me how to fix problems on my little Honda as they came along. Otherwise, I'd have been fucked. Locating the fuse box under the hood I started pulling fuses until I found the one that had blown. Of course, I didn't have spare fuses in my car, like a responsible, prepared adult would. So, I did what I do best, I improvised.

After pulling a good fuse from another slot, I plugged it into the one that had blown silently praying the stolen fuse wasn't for anything important. Running back to the driver's seat, I turned over the engine once more and sure as shit I could move the shifter into gear. I hopped out again and replaced fuse box lid, slammed the hood and dove back into my car, tearing out of there like a bat out of Hell.

***

I walked into my house, set my keys down on the side table, and dropped the embarrassingly small box of personal effects from my desk by the door. After working for the same woman for nearly three years I should have had more to show for it than a couple of framed pictures, a coffee mug, and joke of the day calendar.

There was a definite odor in the house. It seemed like it was probably coming from the kitchen, maybe. Snatching the room spray I spritzed it in the direction of the kitchen while running away backwards and up the stairs in an effort to avoid the smell following me.

No I wasn't depressed. I was just extremely lazy. It wasn't that I didn't know I had some sort of organism growing in my sink and its second cousin chillin' in my fridge, I did. I wasn't in denial. I was well aware I lived like a frat boy. The thing was, I just didn't give a fuck.

Flinging myself on the bed in my best impression of a Disney princess, I contemplated my situation. I had gotten my final paycheck today which was a little over a weeks' worth of pay. That, coupled with my savings, meant I had exactly $1,726.03 in my bank account and a credit card that was $200 away from being maxed out. Enough to pay for next month's rent but not enough to cover my car payment, insurance, cell phone bill, electricity, not to mention food and gas for longer than a month.

With a groan, I rolled onto my back and stared at the ceiling, my head spinning. I loved my condo, the thought of having to give it up made my stomach churn. My house may have been messy, but it was mine. Living on my own the last two years had been awesome, if not lonely sometimes. I'd finally felt like a real adult, not just someone playing grown up. Now I was going backwards. I had no idea what I was going to do and laying on my bed alone and staring at my ceiling fan was not going to help solve anything.

I needed my girls, they'd fix this. As any twenty-something woman, can attest to, your girlfriends are your tribunal. Nothing can be decided without their input, nothing. Should you give that guy that totally passed gas on the first date a second chance? *Ask your girlfriends.* Are you a horrible person if you check 'no' when asked to donate a dollar to kids with cancer at the grocery store? *Ask your girlfriends.* Should you believe him when he tells you 'it slipped'? *Ask your girlfriends.* Can you burn your nipples in a tanning bed? *Ask your girlfriends.* Is telling someone to 'suck my dick' at work considered sexual harassment even though you don't actually have a dick? *Ask your girlfriends.* Women analyze everything. It's what we do, and our favorite past time was analyzing in a group.

I blindly patted next to myself on the bed searching for my phone because picking up my head to actually look was far too difficult an act to manage in my current state. I scrolled through my recent calls looking for Alex's number, since she was the only one out of my friends that would be available at ten in the morning on a Thursday.

As soon as I pressed the call button the phone slipped out of my hand and fell directly on my face, corner first. "Arg, fuck, bitch, motherfucking cocksucker!" I yelled as I held my eye and wondered, not for the first time, what the hell I did to have karma fucking me so hard today.

"Hello?" Alex's voice called out faintly from my phone that must have bounced off the bed after it tried to blind me for life. I rolled to the edge of the bed because my newly unemployed depression was still sucking every ounce of energy from me, and picked up the phone.

"Hey," I said in a huff, falling onto my back once again.

"What happened?" Alex's husky voice filtered through the line.

"What makes you think something happened?" I asked feeling kind of put out that she already knew something was up and I wouldn't get to enjoy the shock and awe of my announcement.

"You're calling me when you're supposed to be at work and you sound like someone just kicked your puppy."

"I don't have a puppy."

"My point exactly, so spill," she said with an exasperated sigh.

"I got canned."

"What the fuck? Why? That old wench finally killed someone and you refused to help her bury the body, huh?"

I laughed. Alex was definitely the imaginative one of the bunch, the shit that girl came up with sometimes. "No, I was late again."

"Oh, well then you deserved it. If you worked for me, I would have fired you a long time ago."

"Thanks for the vote of confidence. I had a good excuse," I tried to defend myself, and failed miserably because Alex was a no bullshit woman. She was the friend that would tell you without hesitation or shame that yes, that outfit did, in fact, make you look fat.

"No, you didn't. And even if you did have a good excuse this time, you didn't the dozen other times you were late. That being said, it still sucks and I'm sorry."

"Boo, I hate it when you're right."

"I'm always right. So, we boozing it up tonight?"

"Hell yes. I want to get drunk and make major life decisions, because that's what being an adult is all about, right?"

"Sounds like a plan. Hang on a sec," Alex said distractedly and I could hear her talking to someone through the muffled speaker. "Hey, my first appointment of the day just cancelled. Why don't you get your ass down here and we can work on your side? A little ink therapy will do you good."

"Be there in ten," I said quickly, all earlier laziness burned away with the thought of getting under the needle.

"Come around the back when you get here, the front isn't open yet."

"That's what she said."

"Dumbass," Alex said through a laugh.

"Hey," I caught her just before she hung up. "Thanks."

"Love you too babe, now get your ass down here and in my chair."

***

The buzzing of the needle lulled me into a calm Zen-like state. Yeah fucking right, it hurt like a bitch. I don't care what anyone says about tattoos, color is the worst. The repetitive strokes with multiple needles to blend the colors felt like scrubbing a sunburn with a Brillo pad. That being said, the end result was totally worth it.

Besides, Alex would kick my ass if I acted like a little bitch in her chair and I would never get a free tattoo again. She was a total hard ass when it came to clients. She could handle the cringing and frequent breaks of a newbie but if you started crying or fidgeting in her chair she'd kick your ass out until you could come back and act like a fucking adult. She was not about to let some wiggly client fuck up her work, she had a reputation to uphold.

Alex was doing the color on my Alice in Wonderland inspired side piece. It was huge, spanning from just below my hip to my ribcage. The piece was kind of a hodgepodge of images from the story, a pocket watch, the Mad Hatter's top hat, the Queen of Hearts, a tea pot and cup, and a little vile with a 'drink me' tag. All the images were brought together with flowers and a ribbon intertwined through the entire piece that featured my favorite quote 'I knew who I was this morning but I've changed a few times since then'. It wasn't my first tattoo, but it was by far my biggest. Being best friends with one of the best tattoo artists in town definitely had its perks.

"So what happened with Tony?" Alex asked after an hour of silence.

"Who?"

"Uh, the guy you went out with last night?"

I started laughing hysterically. Jesus, at least I had the 'y' right.

"What the fuck? That bad huh?"

"No, just…" I broke out in another fit of giggles. After finally catching my breath, I answered, "I thought his name was Tommy."

"He must not have made much of an impression," she mumbled as she loaded the needle with color.

"Oh he made an impression, just not a very good one."

"Dude, stop being cryptic and tell me what happened."

"Fine, from what I can remember, we hit it off fine at the bar and went back to his place..."

"Wait, you slept with this guy and couldn't even remember his name?"

"Alejandra Esmeralda Cortez, the best friend code states that you are not allowed to judge me for my questionable behavior."

"I'm not judging, I'm clarifying. There's a difference," She said blowing a stray piece of fire-engine red hair off her face.

"Whatever, anyways, we went back to his place and started drinking whiskey and watching *Star Trek*— "

"Jesus, you are such a fucking nerd, even your hook ups are nerdy," Alex laughed.

"Fuck you, Captain Kirk is a hot piece of ass. Are you going to let me finish?"

"As soon as you tell me you're referring to Chris Pine and not William Shatner."

"Shatner was a total babe back in the day!"

"You have a weird obsession with old guys, have you seen a psychologist for your daddy issues?"

"It's not a weird obsession, they just don't make men like they used to. That doesn't mean I want to diddle some old guy's nutsack," I said indignantly.

"Whoa! Way more information than I needed to know about my little sister!" Kellen exclaimed coming around the corner.

"Hey big brother, what are you doing here?" I asked as he took a seat across from me. My brother and I looked a lot alike, same brown hair and matching eyes, but he was about a foot taller than me and built like a lumberjack.

"Alex texted me and said you were having a bad day. I just wanted to stop by and make sure you were okay." Kellen was talking to me, but his eyes kept darting to where I knew Alex was working.

I loved my brother, he was the best person I knew, but he was shit at hiding his feelings. He'd been in love with my best friend for years, but was far too chicken shit to ever make a move. I had tried to push the relationship in college, but had given up when Kellen locked me in a closet until I promised to stop meddling. Figuring that eventually they'd either hook up or my brother would move on, I left it be. As far as I could tell, Alex hadn't even entertained the idea.

"Just having the worst day of my life, no biggie."

Kellen turned his focus back to me, "What? Why?"

"I forgot the name of the guy I hooked up with last night, had to do the walk of shame from his 80s porno apartment, changed for work in a McDonald's bathroom that smelled like a sewer, was late for work and got fired, had to do a second walk of shame from the office with my pathetic box of personal items, blew a fuse in my car, and my house smells funny." I whined.

He just blinked at me for a minute, processing what I'd just told him. "Okay, I'm going to pretend I didn't hear the first part. Do you know what you're going to do? What's your plan?"

I laughed. Typical Kellen, Mr. Fix it. "Nope, I haven't a clue. My plan is to wallow for the rest of the day, drink copious amounts of alcohol tonight and make major life decisions while inebriated. You know, like someone who has their shit together."

Kellen squinted his eyes at me but didn't say anything, I knew it killed him not to be able to jump in and make everything better. But he'd learned long ago that I needed to figure things out for myself, even if it took me falling on my face a few times before I got it right.

"Just let me know if you need help, yeah?" He asked.

"Thank you, but I'll be fine," I said, giving him a half smile. I didn't know how it was going to be fine. My life was a total mess but my pride wouldn't let me lean on my big brother to fight my battles for me. I was twenty-five, I needed to pull up my big girl panties and figure it out on my own.

***

"What am I going to do? I have no savings and I can't afford to stay here. I really love this condo." I said numbly into my wine glass. At this point I didn't know if I was talking to my friends or the wine.

"Why don't we get a place together? I need to get out of my dad's house. It was only supposed to be temporary but I've been there almost a year, it's time," Evie slurred as she popped open another beer.

She'd moved back in with her dad after a particularly shitty relationship, and had yet to find a place of her own. I suspected she didn't want to live alone. I didn't blame her, while having your own space had its perks it did get lonely and for someone like Evie that was not a good thing. She was a social person; she didn't do well alone.

"Oh my God! That's a fantastic idea!" I shouted, sloshing wine all over my hand in my exuberance.

"Riiiight?" Evie drew out the word.

"Alex, what about you? Between the three of us we could rent a house, it would be so fucking awesome!"

Alex quirked her head to the side and contemplated my drunken proposal. She'd had a late client so she had only been at my place an hour and was nowhere near our level of hammered. "Javi's coming back in a few months so I would have to move anyways and the rent is already paid up..." she trailed off thinking it through. Javi was Alex's twin brother, she'd been living in his one-bedroom apartment while he was deployed overseas. It was an arrangement that worked well for them. Alex got free rent and Javi had a home base and a place to keep all of his stuff while he was away, win-win.

"I'm down, let's do it," she said with a nod.

Evie and I squealed in delight and launched ourselves at her. This was going to be perfect. We'd always talked about living together but it had never been the right time.

"Okay, okay, calm the fuck down you psychos. If we're going to do this we need to lay down some ground rules," Alex demanded. Evie and I nodded in agreement, which I was sure in our inebriated state made us look like bobble heads.

After an hour of collaboration, we finally had a list of rules we would follow and the consequences that we would have to endure if we were to break any rules.

House Rules

1. No sex in common areas of the house

2. Boyfriends cannot spend the night more than two nights a week

3. If you aren't coming home, you have to text at least one roommate and let them know

4. No dishes in your room for more than 24 hours ~~(Brian)~~ (Don't be a dick, this is for everyone)

5. Everyone chips in for groceries

6. All utilities will be split three ways

Any and all deviation of the rules will result in public humiliation

Three

Saint Evelyn

Do you ever wake up in the morning and wonder what the hell happened to your life?

My mind jumped into turbo charged mode within the first twenty seconds after I woke up. The details of my life, my problems, goals, successes, and failures flipped through my mind like pages of a book caught in the wind. It was as if my subconscious was giving me a rundown of my shortcomings, just in case I dared try to forget.

My subconscious is a bitch.

Rolling out of bed I tried to stand and immediately fell back down. My head was pounding. Fuck, I really shouldn't drink wine, it always gave me a monster hangover. I didn't have time for a hangover today, I had shit to do.

I had to find a job as soon as possible. Now that I'd been freed of the manacles that were Ms.

Callahan, I was kind of excited. Not being chained to a dead-end job was a blessing. I would go out and find the perfect job, one that I would never be late for because I loved it so much. A job that meant something, a job I could brag about when I went to my high school reunion. Because if I was being honest, aside from making money, that was the real goal.

With renewed energy, I was ready to make this job search my bitch. But first, coffee. Lots and lots of coffee, and maybe a few hundred Aspirin. Maybe some bacon, but after that I was diving head first into the dream job search.

***

I was banging my forehead on the kitchen table when my cell rang. I fumbled with the phone and answered without looking or stopping the steady rhythm of my head connecting with the table. "Hello," I mumbled.

"Uh oh, I take it the job search isn't going too well?" Evie's far too chipper voice came through the speaker.

"This sucks, I've been at it for four hours and all I've managed to do is make my resume look pretty. I haven't even updated it. Unless you count the fifty times I changed my objective. Dude, how is it that I have no idea what I want to do?"

"Just take a break, read a book or something. Get your mind off of it. I'll come over after work and help."

"You don't have to do that," I groaned. I was an adult I should be able to find a job by myself.

"I have some rental listings I want to run by you anyways, it's no big deal."

"Alright. See you in a couple hours," I relented.

***

At four, they tell you you can be anything. At 11, you're only as good as the next standardized test. At 17, your entire future is defined by your SAT scores. At 18, you're expected to decide your future by choosing the college where you begin your journey into adulthood. With each passing year, the people that comprise 'they' become broader. They're the people that tell you what and how you should be, and what you should do to be successful. To achieve what we're all supposed to achieve, power and money. Because that's what everyone wants, right?

What they don't tell you is what to do after. When you can't find a job because there are a million other college grads that just got a business degree. They don't tell you what the hell you're supposed to do with your life when you're twenty-five, overeducated and underqualified. No one ever told you that every job you applied for was going to require experience, not just a degree. All of a sudden the group that has been telling you what to do your entire life is gone, vanished, poof. All of a sudden you're an adult and you have no idea what you're supposed to do with the rest of your life. All of a sudden you're adrift and you have to figure it all out on your own.

'They' can go fuck themselves.

Seven hours into the job search and I was about two minutes from pulling all the hair out of my head and running outside naked and covered in butter. At least that way I'd get a nice padded room, three meals a day and a cute jacket that made me hug myself so I'd never be lonely.

Knocking on my front door pulled me from thoughts of my impending psychotic break. I shuffled like Igor to answer it because I'd been sitting on my right foot for the last hour and my entire leg had fallen asleep. I opened the door to a beaming Evie and a surprised and slightly disgusted Alex.

"Don't look at me like that," I said and turned to shuffle back to my station at the kitchen table, dragging my dead leg behind me.

"What the—" Evie started but Alex cut her off.

"Just ignore it, she's in one of her moods. Say the wrong thing and you'll set her off. The troll version of Briar has taken over; we just have to keep feeding it chocolate and wine and wait it out. The real Briar will eventually resurface."

"I heard that," I growled, she wasn't wrong though. I was in a mood. A very pissy mood.

Plopping down on my chair in front of my computer I groaned in defeat, "This is so hard, why is it so hard?" I asked the room in general.

"Were you rubbing it?" Alex asked nonchalantly.

I tried to stay pissy but I couldn't hold the laughter in. It started as a chuckle, elevated to a giggle, and finally erupted into a full belly laugh until I was bent over, my face was red, and tears were streaming down my cheeks. All my frustration and stress melted away in the presence of my two best friends, they got me. They got my 13-year old boy humor. Because honestly, nothing says friendship like inappropriate penis jokes.

"I love you guys," I declared when I finally caught my breath.

"We know," Alex said, sitting across from me at the table.

"We're going to help you find the most kick ass job. Where's your resume?" Evie asked, getting right down to business.

I slid the laptop over to her, "Here, it's total shit. I should have paid more attention in high school when we did mock resumes," I said burying my head in my hands. I peeked through my fingers only to see Evie cringe slightly, which in turn, caused my despair to reach an all-time low.

"It just needs some polishing, that's all," Evie said with a polite smile, the one that told me she was lying through her teeth and I was destined to flip burgers for the rest of my life. I might as well have Alex tattoo a rose on my left tit and join a prison pen pal group.

"I'm going through an existential crisis," I declared.

"Do you even know what that means?" Alex asked.

"Whatever bitch," I grumbled. "I mean who am I? I'm 25 years old, I should know who the fuck I am, right? There are 16 year olds out there that know who they are and what they want to be, why is it so hard for me to figure it out?"

"Well, you have a Bachelor's degree in human resource management, that's a start," Evie said calmly.

"Right. The problem is, the only experience I have in the real working world is as a personal assistant. No one is going to hire me for an HR position without any experience."

"Let's focus on the positive," Evie instructed. "What you have, are excellent computer skills, exemplary verbal and written skills, and good time management."

"Do you think it's kind of wrong for me to say I have good time management when I got fired from my last job for being late?" I asked, feeling slightly guilty.

"Don't worry about it, no one actually calls references anymore. In this day and age, it's too much of a liability," Evie said, and I nodded my head in agreement.

"What do you mean liability? I don't understand," Alex interrupted.

"Well, the employee could sue them for defamation of character. It doesn't really matter what they said, if the employee thinks it prevented them from getting their new job, they'd have a case. Not many employers will give a reference anymore, so most companies don't bother calling at all," I explained.

"See, that was a perfect HR response," Evie said. "So back to the resume, you can embellish a little bit. Instead of secretary, you where an executive administrative assistant and you managed all of the incoming data reporting. The key is not to over promise; you can't say you're an expert at something if you've never done it. Just exaggerate. Everybody lies on their resume."

I managed a weak smile, but I was discouraged with the whole process. No matter how many pretty words Evie put in my resume, it didn't change the fact that I didn't have any experience in my field of choice. I didn't want to start over with a new company and be the bottom feeder again. Even when I worked for Lady Macbeth I had the most seniority of all the assistants, so I was able to at least boss them around. Life at the bottom sucks balls, and not in a fun way.

"Stop, you're being a little bitch about this. Pull your head out of your ass and get it in the game. We didn't come here to join your pity party, let's get to it," Alex chimed in with her usual no nonsense, get shit done attitude. God, I loved this woman. She always knew how to pull me out of my funk.

"Okay, so where do we start?" I asked, looking from one to the other.

"Don't ask me, I've never written a resume," Alex said with her hands lifted in surrender.

"First, we need to start out with an objective," Evie responded.

"Umm, get a job?"

"Right, 'To find full time employment with a company that encourages growth from within'."

"Whoa, how the fuck did you do that?" I asked completely dumbfounded.

"Like I said, just needs some polishing."

We continued like that for over an hour, combing over every line and by the end Evie had made me seem like an actual professional. It was about as close to a miracle as I'd ever seen, and for the rest of the night I referred to her as Saint Evelyn.

Four

Poor Choices and PT Cruisers

While Saint Evelyn's work on my resume was amazing, it didn't change the fact that I only had three years of professional working experience and a completely unused degree. Most of the jobs I was interested in were looking for at least five years' experience in the HR management field.

So, I did the only thing someone in my situation could do, I went to a fucking temp agency. I hated myself for giving up so early in the game, but I needed cash sooner rather than later. It was possible I could even get hired on permanently somewhere I was temping, and at the very least I could stop stressing about money while I continued to look for something in the HR field on the side.

Alex and I were settled on the back patio celebrating my new placement with the temp agency when the Saint herself came rushing through my sliding glass window.

"I did a bad thing, a VERY, VERY BAD THING!" Evie exclaimed as she paced in front of us.

"What did you do?" I asked genuinely concerned, Evie wasn't prone to freak-outs, that was my territory.

"Ugh! It's so bad, oh my GOD!" She shook her hands out at her sides, almost like she was trying to shake the panic out of her system.

"Dude, here," Alex stood up, slapping the half empty bottle of wine into Evie's hand and forcibly guided her to one of the patio chairs. "Take a drink and tell us what the fuck is going on."

She lifted the bottle to her lips and chugged. "Whoa, this must be bad. I'm grabbing the Fireball," I said.

Evie hated wine, she said it tasted like ass raisins. Whatever the fuck that meant. If whatever was bothering her was serious enough to chug wine from the bottle, then we needed something stronger to get through the night.

It took me less than a minute to run inside and snatch the shot glasses and the bottle of Fireball from the freezer. I set everything on the patio table and poured each of us a shot.

"Bottoms up, bitches!" I said as we clinked glasses and downed the shots.

"Alright, Evie tell us what the fuck is going on," Alex demanded.

Evie took a deep breath, looking at her hands that were resting in her lap, she peeked up at us from under her lashes and cringed. "I- uh, I slept with my boss."

"What?!" I shouted, "How did that even happen?"

"Ugh, we went out for drinks with a few people from work, mostly everyone had left already and I told him that I needed to get going. He offered to walk me to my car since when I got there I had to park around the back of the bar. It just sort of happened. It was an accident!"

"What do you mean it was an accident? Like you tripped and fell on his dick?" Alex questioned.

"I don't know..." Evie grumbled, her head in her hands. She was nearly folded in half in her chair.

"Wait a minute, where did you have sex?" I asked, because things weren't adding up.

"He parked right next to me, his windows are tinted." Evie said into her hands.

Alex gagged, "Eww Evie! I would expect something like that from Briar, but you? Dude he drives a fucking PT cruiser...with flame decals."

"Hey!" I objected, because I would never sleep with a guy who owned a PT cruiser, that's just sad.

"I know! I'm a fucking whore!" Evie called out resting her forehead on the table. "What the hell am I going to do?" she asked and rolled her head to the side to look up at me.

I shrugged, "Was it good?"

Evie didn't say anything, just groaned and buried her face in her arms again.

"It couldn't have been good. Car sex is never as hot as they make it out to be in books and movies, it's awkward and painful. You always end up with a Charlie horse and bruises in the weirdest places." Alex shuddered in disgust.

"It wasn't that bad," Evie started, but then heaved a sigh. "Okay, it was bad. We had to move the car seat out of the way, my head kept hitting the roof of the car, and I'm pretty sure his zipper caused some serious chaffing," she said shifting in her seat uncomfortably.

"Ouch. Wait, isn't he married?" I asked.

"Separated, he just moved into an apartment near the office."

Alex let out a whistle, "Damn girl."

"I know! How am I going to face him tomorrow morning?" Evie asked as she grabbed the Fireball and refilled her shot glass. She downed it and grimaced, "I am so fucked."

Evie worked in a physical therapy clinic as a PT assistant while she was still in school, working towards her Master of Science in Physical Therapy degree. The boss in question, was one of the physical therapists and her direct supervisor.

"Literally," I laughed, because in this kind of situation the only thing you could do was laugh. "Did you at least use protection?"

"Of course, I'm not a complete idiot. The last thing I need to do is get knocked up by my married boss. He already has three fucking kids."

"We're in our mid-twenties, we're supposed to do stupid shit like have sex in public. We just need to find you an appropriate partner to do said stupid shit with," I said.

"Yeah, because hot, available guys are everywhere, right?" Evie asked.

"I know one place we can find some," I said, a plan coming slowly together in my fireball addled brain.

"Where?"

"The internet," I declared like I was announcing that I'd discovered the cure for cancer. It may not have been the cure for cancer but it was the cure for sad vaginas, which was basically the same thing, right?

"Dude, seriously? We cannot be at that point already," Alex complained.

"When was the last time you got laid?" I asked.

"I don't know, a couple months ago."

"Let me rephrase, when was the last time you had good sex?"

"Point taken, what do we do?"

"We are creating profiles for ourselves on whatacatch.com. Apparently, all you have to do is put up a couple cute pictures and answer a few questions and the men will come." I explained, as I clicked away on my phone.

"Fuuuuck, okay. I'm in," Evie reluctantly agreed.

"Yeah okay, how bad can it be?" Alex said.

***

"Holy shit, this is bad. Dude, check this guy out. His profile picture is of him, shirtless, sitting in a computer chair, deep throating a corndog!" Alex exclaimed, as she shoved her phone in my face.

We were two hours and several shots into our online dating experience. Evie was curled up on the floor in front of the T.V. laughing hysterically at a dick pic she'd gotten almost an hour ago. Alex and I were on opposite ends of the couch with a bottle of Fireball between us. We'd long since abandoned the shot glasses and were just taking turns off the bottle.

"No fucking way!" I screamed, and grabbed the phone from her to get a better look since she'd been waving it around like a beauty queen on a Rose Festival float. I had to squint, because it was difficult to focus in my state of intoxication. "His name is Phillip, he's 31, he 'enjoys online role playing games and isn't afraid of a woman that can take control'" I snorted out a laugh, "You know what that means don't you?" I asked, and continued without waiting for a response, "This little tidbit coupled with the profile picture means he lives in his mom's basement and likes to take it up the ass by a dominatrix wearing a strap-on."

"No way!" Evie screamed and then continued to giggle and roll around on the floor.

"I don't know, but it sounds like it could be true."

"You are so much meaner than I ever knew," Alex stated, and stared at me in wonder.

"No, I'm not. You always knew how mean I could be. You've heard how I talk to Knox."

"Hmm, true."

"But seriously, have either of you found anyone worth going out with yet?"

"I've got a potential but I told him I had to go to bed like an hour ago because I'm too drunk to keep a conversation going," Alex said as she thumbed through profiles.

"Meh, not really," Evie called out, when her giggles had finally subsided.

"I'm talking to three guys right now and sexting with another. I'm still in the vetting process so time will tell if they're worth giving my phone number to," I said as I responded to pilotguy777.

"What?!" They both yelled in unison, scrambling over to get a better look.

"You're sexting with a guy already?" Alex shouted two inches from my face.

"Fuck, relax. It's not like I'm going to actually meet him. It's just good practice." I said.

"I've never sexted-ed," Evie stuttered, "I mean, I never sexy-ed. Fuck, you know what I mean! Show me!"

"Here," I said, and pulled up the conversation I was having with deltadave84 so they could read it.

> **Deltadave84:** Hey gorgeous
> **Briarrose15:** Hey yourself, how's your night going?
> **Deltadave84:** Good you?
> **Briarrose15:** Pretty good
> **Deltadave84:** Can I ask you a question and you not get offended?
> **Briarrose15:** I'm not easily offended, shoot
> **Deltadave84:** Do you like it rough?
> **Briarrose15:** Depends on who's giving it

"Oh my God! That's like five messages in, you dirty slut!" Alex shouted, again two inches from my ear.

"Bitch, if you don't stop screaming in my ear I'm going to tell your brother you fucked his commanding officer!"

"You wouldn't!" she gasped.

"Oh, I would. So, shut your trap you whore." I swore, and we continued reading.

Deltadave84: I could give it to you real good

Briarrose15: Details?

Deltadave84: I like to get behind my woman, slap her ass, grab a handful of hair and force her back to arch. Wrap my forearm around her neck and just pound that pussy so goddamn deep over and over again

Deltadave84: Or when we are standing up I make you grab your ankles, pin you up against a wall so you can't wiggle or run away from this big dick. Slam dat ass, drill this big dick so goddamn deep and hard that my neighbors can hear you screaming and your legs start shaking and convulsing and you feel me beating your stomach in.

"Ahh!" This time it was Evie screaming in my ear, "Who the fuck says shit like that?"

"Deltadave84 apparently," I replied, more than a little over the screaming. It was like these women had never dirty talked before, Jesus.

Briarrose15: Damn, you know how to get a girl wet

Deltadave84: Damn straight, I know how to fuck and I never half ass it. You think you can handle this big dick?

Briarrose15: Is it big enough to choke on?

Deltadave84: Oh yeah, I would face and throat fuck you, cum bubbles coming out of your nose

"Whoa!" I said as I read the last reply, "I didn't see that last one. Well that's a little too intense even for me," I said and looked up to see the other girls just staring at me like I'd grown another head. "What?" I asked, completely confused. Evie looked like she was going to be sick and Alex looked like she was going to start worshiping at my feet.

"You are a fucking master," Alex said, her voice full of awe.

"I didn't even really do anything but open the door. He's the one that did all the dirty talking. You've got to admit, it's good material."

Alex nodded her head but didn't say anything.

"I've had it wrong this whole time. Do people really get that detailed?" Evie asked, still looking a bit queasy.

I shrugged, "Some, not all. Fucking calm down. The beauty of the internet is anonymity; you can say whatever to whoever and you don't have to worry about facing them. You just ghost them, at least that's my plan."

"Ghost them?" Evie asked.

"Just stop responding," Alex said.

Evie gave us a confused look, "Isn't that kind of mean?"

"Meh, social niceties kind of go out the window when the term 'cum bubbles' is used." I said, which was totally true. You couldn't expect manners when you were sexting, otherwise it wouldn't be sexting.

Five

Liquid Potatoes?

"Oh my God!" Evie exclaimed, "What the fuck is that? Does it have hair?"

"Dude, how do you even let it get this bad? It looks like a science project; this is fucking disgusting." Alex's voice was muffled from behind her shirt that she'd pulled over her nose and mouth.

"Yeah well, so is your fucking vagina but you don't see me judging your ass for it, do you?"

We had been packing up my kitchen and Evie opened one of the cupboards to find a forgotten sack of potatoes that had nearly liquefied in the dark recesses of my cabinet.

That's where the smell had been coming from.

"You are such a dude," Alex said, as she held out a fresh trash bag so Evie could dispose of the offending potatoes.

"Fuck off, not everyone can be an OCD freak like you."

"Your glassware consists of mason jars."

"Hey! Mason jars are multipurpose; you can drink out of them and use them as storage for leftovers. They're glass so you don't get that weird orange ring when you use Tupperware to store spaghetti sauce." I said with a huff.

"I call bullshit; you have never cleaned out a container that has been sitting in your fridge for over a month. You just throw it away, admit it."

I flipped her off and continued my task of packing my cookware. If it could be called packing. The little tray thing that held the silverware in the drawer wouldn't fit in the box so I'd resorted to dumping the contents of all my drawers into the box haphazardly. I'd organize it when I unpacked.

"You're lucky we love your disgusting ass," Evie commented as she sprayed disinfectant on the puddle of whatever the fuck the rotten potatoes had left behind.

"You're stuck with me," I conceded.

"Alright, I have an hour before I need to be at the shop, so I'm going to head out. We're still on for tomorrow night?" Alex asked.

"Yeah, at the new place," Evie responded, her head buried in the cabinet beneath the microwave.

Evie and I spent the next two hours gutting my kitchen until there were six neatly stacked boxes in the corner and the floors were sparkling. After two weeks of searching, we'd finally found the perfect house in an awesome neighborhood. Lots of young people, cool shops and it was only a block from our favorite bar. Alex was moving in next weekend but I had to be out of my place by tomorrow. My landlord had been nice enough to accept a two week notice instead of the usual 30 days since she had other tenants on a waiting list and available to move in right away. It also helped that I was on a month to month lease so there weren't any fees to break a lease early.

Evie had already moved her stuff in the day before. She didn't have all the house ware stuff that I did since she'd left all that shit with jackass Jake when she'd left him and moved back in with her dad. Things were progressing nicely; I hadn't found my dream job yet, but I would be starting my first temp assignment Monday. That would pay the bills until I found something more permanent.

My thoughts were interrupted by the sound of the front door opening and boots thudding in the entryway, "Briar?"

"In here," I called out, and lifted my head from where I was tying off the last garbage bag in time to see Kellen round the corner with his best friend Knox right behind him.

Those two had been attached at the hip since middle school. Wherever one went the other followed, kind of like Evie, Alex, and I. Travis Knox or Knox as his friends called him, was a giant. He stood six-four and over two hundred pounds of straight up muscle with blue eyes and shaggy blonde hair. He always looked like he hadn't shaved in a couple of days despite my constant reminders that flesh colored beards were beyond creepy.

While I could admit that he was hot, he'd been the bane of my existence since I was twelve years old and having an archenemy for that long was a hard habit to break. Although, over the years our relationship had progressed from plotting each other's untimely deaths to the much friendlier verbal sparring matches and occasional practical joke.

"Whoa," Knox exclaimed. "This is the cleanest I've seen this place since we moved you in two years ago."

"Thanks," Evie replied before I had a chance. It was true though, if it had been up to me I would've thrown everything in garbage bags and called it a day. I had paid a non-refundable cleaning deposit for a reason, why should I have to scrub the floors when I'd already paid to have someone else do it for me? But Evie wouldn't listen to reason.

Knox laughed, "Yeah, we know it's all you, Evie. Briar doesn't even own a mop."

"Hey! I have a Swiffer!"

"Not the same thing," Kellen responded with a shake of his head like it was a ridiculous comparison. "Come on, we brought the truck. Let's get this shit loaded. We only have a few hours of daylight left."

***

"I can't believe I have this much shit," I said as we unloaded the final box from the truck. It took a 14 foot U-Haul and Knox's monster truck to get everything.

"I can. I just spent the last four hours hauling it across town." Knox said as he wiped sweat off his face with the front of his shirt, which of course revealed an awesome set of abs. I could practically hear the straight females in the neighborhood swooning. Fucking show off.

"Shut it, cupcake," I said with an eye roll. He hated it when I call him that, which was precisely why I did it. He just growled in response, and I scowled back at him. If he wasn't my brother's best friend and a royal pain in my ass, I might've thought it was sexy. I was such a fucking liar. It was totally sexy but even the thought of touching man-whore Knox made me queasy and itching to run for the nearest bottle of antibiotics, pun intended.

"Alright kids," Kellen, always the peacemaker, intervened before we could go at each other's throats. "We're on shift tomorrow so we need to get home and get some shut eye. Are you good here?"

"Yeah, we're good. Thanks for your help today," I said and leaned in to give him a hug.

"Pfft, help? We did all the work!" Knox shouted from the driver seat of his jacked-up truck.

I flipped him off and called out, "Yeah, yeah, yeah, pencil dick!"

"Pencil dick?" he questioned, and made a move like he was grabbing his junk, "You couldn't handle what I'm working with, sweetheart!"

"Your truck says otherwise!" I screamed as he pulled out onto the road.

"Come on, do you guys have to do that shit?" Kellen asked with a sigh.

"He started it."

"Whatever," he said shaking his head.

"You know it'll never end. We'll be ninety in the nursing home and I'll still hide his dentures, it's just the way we operate."

"At least it's free entertainment. Okay, I'm gone, love you!" he shouted and climbed into the U-Haul.

"Love you back!" I yelled and jogged up the stairs to the front porch.

The last box was labeled for my room so I headed down the hall in that direction. I hadn't actually gone into my room all day. Mainly because Knox was right. I'd stayed outside to hand boxes to the guys and made them do the actual work of taking them into the house. When I shoved open the door to my bedroom my only thought was that I was going to kill him. I was going to kill him so fucking hard.

Knox had effectively sealed his fate of a slow and torturous death by wallpapering my entire room in pictures of Nicholas Cage. I knew it was him because Kellen would never take the time. There were even pictures taped to a string that had been hung up across the room like a banner.

Game on motherfucker.

Tearing down the photos, I started dreaming up ways to get him back. Knox and I had spent the majority of our teen years pranking each other but as we got older the pranks got fewer and farther between. But now he'd thrown down the gauntlet and we weren't kids anymore. I had a few things up my sleeve.

Six

Prank Calls and Classified Ads

New job, new place, new me. That was my new mantra.

I took a deep breath and stared up at the giant building where I'd be working as a customer service agent. Hopefully not for too long, but I was determined to make the best of it. Yesterday I'd moved into an awesome house with my best friends and today, a new job.

Look at me adulting all over the place. I had this.

***

I so didn't have this.

First, there was a half hour of password and program set ups, followed by an hour-long HR video. Then, my new boss Janis, thrust a set of scripts at me and turned on my desk phone so that I was connected to the main call hub like everyone else in the room. I muddled my way through the first few callers, and prayed that I'd gotten them transferred to the right department.

By the time my ninth call came in I felt like I was starting to get the hang of it. That is until all that greeted me on the other end of the phone was heavy breathing. I repeated my greeting, and nothing, just more breathing. The HR video specifically stated we were not allowed to hang up on any customer, no matter what. I repeated my greeting for a third time, glancing around at my co-workers for help. I could tell someone was there but they weren't saying anything.

"Hello?" I asked again, and the breathing on the other end sped up.

What the fuck?

"What are you wearing?" a gravelly voice asked, and not the sexy kind of gravely. I'm talking old pervert driving a van with blacked out windows who smokes two packs a day gravely.

"Excuse me?" I asked incredulously. Serena, the girl in the cube next to me must have seen the horror on my face because she put her call on hold and rolled over to me.

"Pervert?" she asked between smacks of her gum.

58

All I could do was nod.

How did she know?

"Pshh, girl it happens all the time, just hang up."

"But, I thought…"

"Doesn't count when it's a pervert."

"Umm, okay." I said and disconnected the call. Not long after, my phone rang with another call.

The entire day continued like that. I got another four pervert calls, which according to Serena was on the low end.

How did I not know this was a thing?

I was definitely going to need a drink after today, and maybe I'd wash my ears out with bleach.

***

On my way home, I fell back on my tried and true stress relief method, plotting ways to make Knox's life a living hell. I needed to come up with something epic, something that would preferably make him cry.

I sat down at the kitchen island with my laptop as soon as I got home and pulled up Craigslist. Clicking over to the casual encounters link I perused the M4M posts to get some inspiration. A half hour later I'd seen more dicks than a whore at the playboy mansion. The shit these guys said in some of the posts were probably illegal in twelve states.

Glancing at the clock I noticed it was almost seven, Evie would be home soon from class so I had to hurry. She was too much of a softy, if she saw what I was doing she'd probably feel bad and tell Knox. I quickly set up an account using the e-mail address I'd created years ago for pranks such as these and quickly typed out a post keeping it short and dirty.

Young, ripped, hottie looking to suck cock tonight, always swallows. Can host. Any age. Discreet.

I left Knox's real phone number at the bottom of the post with a request for dick pics. Posting the ad with a flourish, I sat back and admired my handy work. It was just a matter of time before Knox started getting random dicks flooding his inbox. He'd figure out it was me pretty quickly, and while I was sure my fun would be short lived, it would be epic.

Was I a terrible person for catfishing? Probably. Did I care? Not one fucking bit.

Seven

Nancy's and Necrophelia

Online dating is bullshit. Total and complete bullshit. I'd talked to over thirty guys and been out with a total of four of them in the past three weeks and I'd come to the conclusion that all men suck.

There are five kinds of men you find online:

First, you have the unemployed or under employed loser. I'm talking the thirty-year-old who is still living in his parent's basement and working as a petroleum transfer technician aka a gas attendant. (Yeah we have those in Oregon. We are far too granola to risk getting fossil fuel on our hands.)

Second, is the 'I just want to fuck' guy. He doesn't need to know your name or even what you look like. This guy sends a blanket message to as many women as possible and just sits back to see who bites.

The third type of guy is a winner, he's the ex-con/ex-drug addict. Not that there's anything wrong with having past vices, but if you feel the need to proclaim them to the world, you're not ready for a relationship. You can use keywords in his profile to pick him out, things like 'I focus on the future not the past', 'I like to stay positive and I'm goal oriented'. Yeah buddy I know; you're talking about your next NA chip. The absolute telltale sign for these guys is the adamant 'I DO NOT do drugs!' or 'I need a girl that will keep me focused on my goals'. Dude, you don't need a girlfriend, you need a sponsor.

The fourth is the hopeless romantic. This guy watches way too many Nicholas Sparks movies and his biological clock is a tickin'. Most likely some bitch broke his heart and now he's on the search for anyone to pin down so he never has to be lonely again. This guy is going to let it all hang out in his profile. Identifying himself as 'looking for someone to marry' or 'looking for my forever'. If you see this, back click, block, swipe left, whatever the online equivalent to run in the opposite direction is, because this guy is a stage five clinger.

The fifth and final guy is absolutely perfect on paper, cute, interesting and even has a funny quip or two on his profile. Most of the time he's either not interested, can't hold an actual conversation, or has been inactive for over a year because he found the love of his life and you missed your fucking chance. If he falls into the small percentage that are still actually available and interested, then you meet him and if it's not on the first date then by the third he'll show you his crazy and once again you're back to square one.

***

My first date from my online profile was a few days after the epic sexting session with Deltadave84. No I did not go out with him, I ghosted his ass like Casper. Instead, I went out with Paul the software engineer. He was tall and broad, just like I liked them, and according to his profile he enjoyed the outdoors and boxed for fun. We met at Murphy's since I felt more comfortable on my own turf. I mean, for all I knew this guy could be Ted Bundy reincarnate.

I had a system with the girls, if I didn't text them the all clear within fifteen minutes they'd send in the cavalry. No such alert was needed. In fact, the date was kind of boring. He wasn't nearly as ripped as his pictures led you to believe and he was much funnier online. We went through the regular niceties and first date questions, where do you work, what do you like to do for fun, what's your family like, etc. I had exactly two beers because I needed to have my wits about me, I didn't want a repeat of the last time I'd met a date there.

Afterwards, he walked me to my car like a gentleman, which totally earned him bonus points in my book. But things took a turn for the disgusting when he leaned in to kiss me goodbye and sneezed right in my face. Not just a little sneeze, nope, it was juicy. There was actual snot and spit on my face. Needless to say, he did not get a call for a second date.

I had two more dates after Paul, which also did not go beyond the first meeting. Jack the wind turbine technician who I found out had a three-month old baby. Dude, if your kid is still on the tit you should not be dating, that just screams unfinished business. Then there was Matt, who actually lived in his parent's basement and failed to mention that before we met.

My latest endeavor into online dating was the pilot, Jared. He actually seemed pretty perfect. Cute, funny, and had his own place. He flew internationally so he was gone for a week and back for a week which suited my needs precisely. Who doesn't want a guy that is only in town two weeks a month? It's like the perfect set up. I actually went on three dates with him. The first two were great; we laughed and talked for hours. He was a total gentleman. I offered to pay and he refused, although politely, which was awesome because I was totally broke.

The strange thing about the first two dates was that he didn't kiss me. I figured he wanted to take things slow, we were strangers after all. Instead he hugged me goodbye both times, which was no big deal, except for the way he hugged me.

The only way to describe it was a creepy uncle hug. You know the one where it's just a little too tight, lasts a little too long, and there may have been some hair sniffing involved. Yeah it was weird, but I ignored the red flag. I mean, maybe no one ever told him he was a creepy hugger.

Things went south on our third date. We were shooting pool and having a few drinks at a bar downtown. Which I knew from previous conversation, wasn't far from his apartment, so I wasn't exactly surprised when he invited me back to his place. I actually kind of expected it, it was the third date and all, I was bound to get some, right?

We made the short walk from the bar to his building. I was stunned when we walked through pristine glass doors and into a lavish lobby. Marble floors led to a front desk manned by a uniformed security guard and a waterfall ran the entire length of one slate wall.

Jackpot!

Hold the Kanye, I'd never been a gold digger. However, after dating countless losers, I was ready for a guy who had his shit together and wasn't going to ask to borrow money from me three months into the relationship. We got into the elevator and made our way to the 23rd floor, the building was uber modern, all sleek lines and polished concrete with glass everywhere.

He led me into his apartment, which wasn't huge but the view totally made up for the small space. Of course, being a bachelor, his furniture consisted of a black leather couch and a huge entertainment system.

The guy loved his gadgets.

"Watch this," he said excitedly as he started fiddling with the iPad that controlled his T.V., stereo, and the lights he had mounted behind the T.V. and surround sound speakers. "They're LED lights, the kind that change color and pulse with the beat of the music," he said, the sound of The Eagles drifted through the speakers.

Dude, Hotel California is not a sexy time song, I love The Eagles as much as the next person but just, no. Again, I ignored the red flag and continued on, no one was perfect. I continued to push down the uneasy feeling, but then things went from weird to oh my God this can't be happening.

"Have a seat, I want to show you something," he said pulling up a website on his T.V. (using his wireless keyboard of course) even worse was that he didn't type in the website. Oh, no, it was on his favorites list, right on top in fact.

It was a fetish social networking site. A place where you could connect with other people who had the same fetishes as you and share pictures and videos. It was basically Facebook with kinky amateur porn. Now, I'm not saying it's bad, you do you boo boo. In any other situation, I would probably think it was cool, but to pull this up on a third date with a woman whom you haven't even kissed throws you straight in the coo coo for coco puffs category.

At this point I was ready to bolt but I needed to find an excuse, so I kept him talking and prayed he didn't try to get physical. This was where I went wrong. I should have said fuck being polite and booked it as soon as things started to turn. Because the more he talked, the creepier he got.

We ended up discussing different fetishes, and I was trying to keep things clinical, opting for more of an intellectual discussion. Of course, that didn't last long when he launched into an explanation of his own kink, "I like rope play, a little bondage can be fun," he said. Pretty tame, right? Wrong. Because he leaned in and followed it up with, "I can't wait to tie you up and watch you turn blue."

What. The. Fuck.

That is not bondage bro, that's necrophilia. There was nothing I could possibly say in response so I just smiled curtly and started looking around for a weapon. Thanks to the minimal furnishings the only thing within arm's reach was a Dyson fan which wasn't going to do shit.

Mercifully, he chose that moment to use the restroom. I quickly slipped on my shoes, grabbed my purse, and was halfway to the door when he caught me in the hallway.

"Where you off to?" he slurred slightly.

"I uh, need to get up in a few hours," I said, continuing towards the door.

"Oh, sure, I'll walk you to your car."

"You don't have to do that, I'll be fine, really."

"I'm not going to let you walk to your car by yourself, it's the middle of the night," he argued.

Seriously? This is the same guy that let me walk to my car by myself in the rain after our second date because he was running late to meet up with his friends. Okay, so maybe there were more red flags than I had initially been willing to admit.

It was the most excruciating elevator ride of my life, he knew I was freaked out, he had to know. I mean there was no way he didn't know how slasher-flick rapey he was. As soon as we got out onto the street I felt safe.

Who in their right mind feels safe on the street at four in the morning? Apparently, I do.

After a stilted conversation and some speed walking on my part, we got to my car. I tried to get away with a wave but he wasn't having it. Nope he leaned in for, you guessed it, a creepy uncle hug. Only this time when he pulled away he dived back in for a kiss. Even though it made my skin crawl, I let him kiss me. I figured it would be easier to kiss him and get the fuck gone than to have a conversation about why I didn't want to kiss him.

But for the millionth time that night, I was wrong. It was worse, so much worse than I could have ever imagined. It was like the cure for cancer was lodged in my throat and the only way to save mankind was for him to fish it out with his tongue. I managed to get in my car after his assault on my tonsils only to have him knocking on my window as soon as I closed the door. I rolled down the window thinking he was going to ask me out again or something but he lunged into the car and stabbed at my mouth with his tongue until I let him in again. After the second worst kiss of my life in just as many minutes I was over being nice. As soon as his body cleared the window I threw my car into reverse and hauled ass out of the garage.

Which is why I was curled up on the couch eating a pint of Ben and Jerry's with a merlot chaser and swiping left like a madwoman on a Friday night. With each disappointing profile, I sunk deeper into despair.

My internal commentary had been entertaining when I'd started an hour ago, but now it was just depressing. Too tall, too tan, not enough teeth, wearing tie dye, crazy eyes, dick pic—eww! It wasn't even a good looking wang, it was two different colors and crooked! I would never understand a man's need to constantly display his genitals. I threw my phone to the other side of the couch and got up to dispose of the evidence of eating my feelings and top off my wine glass.

If there was one thing in my life that never let me down it was wine. I realized that deep self-reflection was not something that was supposed to be done under the influence of copious amounts of Cherry Garcia and alcohol but I'd never been one for rules. So, I sat in the dark, alone in my living room on a Friday night and contemplated the state of my life.

I'd completed step one in my 'get your shit together' plan. Acquiring a new place to live. It was fantastic, I loved my girls and getting to see them all the time was awesome. However, now that we lived together, when I was home alone I felt twice as lonely as I used to. At least when I had my own place and I was by myself I could pretend my friends were at home doing the same thing instead of out enjoying their lives while I moped around about a series of unbelievably shitty dates.

I was still working on the second step; I had found a job, but I hated it. Being a temp paid well enough to afford the basic necessities, but I was still on the lookout for my dream job.

The last step was a new me, but since I had no fucking clue what that even meant it would have to wait until my job situation was solid. No need to get ahead of myself, right?

Eight

Chocolate Crossed Lovers

"Hi," a pathetic whimper travelled through the phone line.

"Evelyn? Babe, what's wrong?"

"I'm so fucking stupid," she sniffled.

"What happened?"

"He lied to me!" she wailed.

"Jesus, Evie," I groaned.

More sobbing came from the other end of the line.

"That's it, be at the house in 30," I instructed and disconnected the call. Scrolling through my recent calls I dialed Alex. She picked up on the first ring.

"Alex's whore house, you got the dough, we got the ho. How can I help you?"

"I'm calling in a DEFCON 1 situation. Be at the house in thirty."

"Shit, Evie?"

"Ding, ding, ding! We have a winner," I said.

"Jesus, fuck me! I've got a consultation in five, shouldn't be more than twenty minutes. I'll head over after. Need me to pick anything up on the way?"

"Nah, I'm headed to the store now to get supplies. I'll see you when you get to the house."

"Okay, don't start without me."

"Wouldn't dream of it, love," I replied and ended the call just as I was pulling into the Fred Meyer parking lot.

Stowing my phone in my purse I climbed out of my car and headed for the entrance of the store. It was going to be a long night.

Grabbing a cart, I bee lined it for the produce section only to discover six feet into the journey that I had selected the cart with the squeaky wheel. It kept getting stuck and then spinning instead of rolling, making it nearly impossible to navigate with. Deciding that I didn't have the time to circle back and change it out I pushed forward with a grunt and practically dragged the damn cart through the aisles. I didn't have time to fuck around. I needed to get in and out as fast as possible. Snatching a few limes, I made my way to the frozen foods section and picked up pizza and six different kinds of ice cream.

I'd never actually been dumped myself, but I'd coached Evie and occasionally Alex through enough breakups to know the protocol by heart.

Pizza, ice cream, cookies, and booze. Not particularly in that order, started out the night. The liquor and junk food were accompanied by a good two-hour rant and men-bashing session followed by a movie. If it was Alex going through a breakup the gorier the movie the better. For Evie on the other hand, it was Nicholas Sparks or nothing. Alex was more of the angry, shoot 'em up, let's hate the world for a few days dumpee. Although, come to think of it, Alex had only been dumped once. The other breakup parties for her revolved around her breaking it off with a fuck buddy and being depressed about the lack of regular sex. Whereas Evie needed to scream and cry it out before she pulled herself together and moved on. I had no idea what I would need should the day ever come that I got dumped. In a way, I was kind of jealous of my friends. Not that I wanted to feel rejected, I just felt like I was kind of missing out on a huge part of life.

Lost in my thoughts while I scanned the shelves for the fudge covered Oreos I knew Evie would want, I didn't see the cart stopped in front of me or the guy standing behind it until I plowed into his heels.

"Ouch, shit!"

"Fuck me! I'm so sorry! That was totally my fault, I wasn't watching where I was going," I called out to the guy who I'd smashed into. He was bent over rubbing his ankles, his hood up and head tilted down so I wouldn't see his face.

"Usually I make a lady buy me dinner first," he said as he straightened out and gave me a onceover, "but for you I think I could make an exception."

It took me a second to catch up with his remark and remember what I'd said to prompt it. I laughed loudly, "Jesus, where are my manners? I should at least ask your name before I demand to be ravaged."

"Pfft, names are overrated."

"I disagree; how will I know what to call out while in the throes of passion?"

"God will do just fine, Master if you're feeling frisky," he smiled at me then, a full toothed, eye crinkling smile.

What was that? Oh, right, that was the sound of me swooning all over aisle eight.

I laughed again, albeit somewhat nervously. Not having a witty retort at the ready I gave up the playful banter, "In all seriousness, I am so sorry. I totally wasn't paying attention to where I was going."

"No worries, I may walk with a limp for the rest of my life but at least I'll do it knowing a beautiful girl caused it. What were you looking for so hard anyways?"

"Fudge covered Oreos,"

"Wait a minute," He narrowed his light eyes on me, I couldn't tell if they were green or blue from this distance. "Milk chocolate or white?"

"Dude, white chocolate all the way."

"Damn, I thought for a minute you might be my soul mate. But no soul mate of mine would prefer white chocolate, that shit is disgusting. It's milk chocolate or nothing."

"You'd let something as trivial as chocolate preference get in the way of true love?"

"Chocolate is not trivial. It's a major food group. It's a shame really, we could have had a wonderful life together."

"You're right, it would be like the Willy Wonka version of Romeo and Juliet. It's best if we end our affair now before someone ends up dead."

It was his turn to laugh. He threw his head back so hard his hood slipped off revealing a head of slightly messy, bright red hair.

OMG he's a motherfucking ginger!

I took a minute to mentally catalog this guy, stubble, gray hoodie, graphic tee, faded jeans, and Converse, total hipster. The only thing he was missing was black framed glasses.

He shook his head as he continued to chuckle and scanned the shelves. "Here they are," he said as he reached up and snatched a box for himself. I moved to follow his lead and grab my box but it was just out of reach. He laughed from behind me.

"A little help?" I asked over my shoulder as I continued to try in vain to activate my go-go-gadget arm.

"First you try to kill me with your cart and now you want my help?"

"Please?" I asked in my sweetest voice even going as far as batting my eyelashes at him.

"Whoa! I've known you for all of five minutes and I can already tell that is not a natural move for you. If I help you will you promise never to do that again?"

"Fuck off!"

"See that seems much more natural. Here," he said and moved to stand behind me. He reached up and grabbed the box from the top shelf, his body ever so slightly brushing against mine in the process. Backing away slightly he handed me the box. He was standing unusually close for a stranger but it gave me a better chance to take him in. He was hot in an unsuspecting way. His ears stuck out slightly from his disheveled hair and he had freckles dotted across his nose. He was fair but not ghostly. When my eyes locked on his I could see they were definitely green. He cleared his throat and stepped away. Glancing around, he caught sight of my cart. "That's some heavy artillery you've got there, planning to feed an army of sad cat ladies?"

"Something like that. Breakup party."

"Ah, I see."

"Not mine," I rushed to said.

Shit, that sounded desperate.

"My best friend just got dumped, had to get supplies," I clarified.

Smooth, Briar. Real fucking smooth.

"My sister does the same thing with her girlfriends. Didn't realize it was a thing."

"Yeah, kind of universal, I guess."

This is getting awkward. Abort, abort!

I pulled out my phone and looked at the time, "Shit, I gotta go. It was nice meeting you…"

"Reid," he said and stuck out his hand.

I took it, "Briar."

"It was nice to meet you Briar, my chocolate crossed lover," he said bringing his lips down to the back of my hand and gently released it, turning to his cart. Just before he turned down the next aisle he called over his shoulder, "Hope your friend feels better!"

I stood in middle of the aisle for a minute stunned. He'd kissed my hand and he didn't even ask for my number.

What the fuck? What an asshat!

You don't just have that kind of easy banter with anyone, that shit is rare. Was he serious about the chocolate thing? I shook my head in confusion. I didn't have time to worry about the cute stranger, I was running late and Evie was probably already at the house. Rushing to the self-checkout I hurriedly rang up my items. I caught sight of orange hair over the top of one of the magazine racks but quickly averted my eyes. The last thing I needed was jerk face catching me staring at him.

I heaved the derelict cart across the parking lot and loaded my groceries into the trunk at record speed. I spun around to the cart return, because only assholes who've never worked in retail would dare leave their cart on the curb. I was halfway to the corral when a dented, spray painted pickup started to reverse, right into me.

"Hey asshole! I'm walking here, try looking in your fucking mirror next time!" I shouted and slapped a hand on the tailgate. The truck lurched to a stop, the brakes grinding and elicited a screeching wail. I saw the guy behind the wheel throw up his hands in an apologetic gesture.

"Whatever," I mumbled under my breath and cleared the ten feet to the cart return. When I turned to walk back to my car the truck had pulled out of the parking space. The driver was waiting for me to cross, I looked through the windshield and recognized the guy from the aisle. He gave me a close-lipped smile and waved. I glared back and stomped to my car. Not only had he totally blown me off, he'd tried to run me over. Jackass.

Nine

Dr. Douchebag

Evie was sitting in her car when I got home. I cursed the stupid jackass for making me late to meet my friend. I parked next to Evie's cherry red Mini Cooper in front of the house and risked a glance at her. She was sitting in the driver seat with her head in her hands. I could hear the man-hating music she was blaring from inside my own car.

It's going to be a long night.

Jumping out of my Honda I hurried to load all the bags on one arm, because two trips were for punk bitches. Evie slinked out of her car and followed me up the walk. My arm shook with exertion and I leaned my upper body to the other side in an effort to keep myself from falling over from the weight of the cornucopia of junk food I was hauling. By some act of God, I was able to unlock the door and get the groceries on the counter before my arm went completely dead.

"You want something to drink?" I asked turning to look at Evie who'd followed me into the house silently. I was surprised when I saw her standing in front of the fridge, beer in hand and tears streaming down her face. Without another word, she popped the top and plopped down on one of the barstools on the opposite side of the island from where I was standing. I went about my business unloading enough refined sugars to throw someone into a diabetic coma without saying another word. She would talk when she wanted to and not a second sooner, especially when it came to a breakup.

I'd been through this routine at least six times since we'd met our freshman year in college. We'd lucked out in the roommate department, at least I did. My reckless behavior coupled with Evie's mother hen qualities made for an interesting first year. I loved our arrangement, especially since I would come back to the dorm after classes and viola my laundry was put away and my bed was made. We ended up rooming together in the dorms for another two years before getting an apartment off campus for our senior year.

"I'm so fucking stupid Briar. Why do I keep doing this to myself?" Evie asked, pulling me out of my reminiscence and bringing my attention back to the task at hand.

"Babe, it's not – "

"I'm here! You bitches better not have started without me," I heard Alex call out from the hallway, immediately followed by the front door slamming and her keys falling into the dish on the side table.

"Calm down, we just got here," I shouted as she rounded the corner, coming into view.

"Dude, what the fuck happened? Do I need to kick someone's ass?" Alex asked as she took the stool next to Evie.

I busied myself pulling out a couple of beers from the fridge as Evie answered her, "I'm an idiot, nothing new there."

"I'm withholding judgment until I hear what happened, so spill," I said handing Alex a beer and parking it on the third stool so Alex and I were sandwiching Evie.

She closed her eyes and took a deep and shaky breath, "So you know how I hooked up with my boss right?"

"Yeah, the separated guy, right?" Alex asked.

"Ha! Joke's on me. He's not separated."

"What in the actual fuck? But I thought he moved into an apartment?

"Apparently, that was his love pad. He didn't just move; he's been keeping that place for over a year."

"Wait, whoa. I thought you just slept with him the one time?" I interjected.

"No," Evie mumbled, "It didn't stop after the first time."

"So you've been sleeping with a married man for over a month without knowing he was married?" I clarified.

"Yup, he told me he wanted to keep his separation from his wife a secret for a while. He didn't want people in the office discussing his personal life. He told me all this shit months ago. Ugh, I can't believe I was so gullible, I just believed him at face value. Then today he said he had to tell me the truth, he couldn't keep it in anymore. You know why? Because the company picnic is next week and his wife is going to be there with their kids."

"Who the fuck does that?" Alex growled.

"That's not even the worst part, you know what he said to me?"

"Oh no. He did not," Alex said, the fury rolling off her in waves had me completely confused.

"What? What am I missing here?" I asked.

"He said that just because he was still with his wife didn't mean we couldn't keep seeing each other. He said he was only staying for the sake of the kids and it would be too expensive to get a divorce but he didn't really love her. He said what we had was different, he said I was special—" Evie cut off her words quickly as a sob bubbled up and escaped her.

"That motherfucker!" Alex yelled, startling both Evie and I. Alex was a force to be reckoned with. Our feisty Latina friend had the temper of a Manchester United fan whose team just lost the world cup due to a bad ref call. When it came to the people she loved she had a hairpin trigger.

"He didn't actually say that, did he?" I asked in disbelief. Evie was in no way a dumb co-ed that would fall for that shit, she was a twenty-five-year-old successful woman. I just didn't understand how someone that knew her would think for a second that she would be okay with being some married guy's side piece.

"Word for word," Evie responded her voice hollow. My heart was breaking for her; I knew what kind of effect this would have on a woman like her. Evie used men to build her self-esteem, she knew it, I knew it. After a few days, she would paint on her façade and pretend to move on, but this would stick with her. She would lament about not being good enough, and this level of rejection would be a huge blow to the little self-confidence she had.

"What did you do?" I asked.

"I punched him in the face and ran away. God, I'm probably going to get fired."

"Did you punch him in front of a bunch of people at work?" Alex asked.

"No, we were in his office. Everyone was gone for the day. It was right after we..." Evie trailed off and my heart sunk into my stomach. This guy was an even bigger douche nozzle than I'd thought.

"Este pendejo, hijo de su pinche madre, voy a matar a ese cabron, vas a ver," Alex rattled off, you knew Alex was pissed when the Spanish came out. "I'm going to kill him!"

"I'll help," I said standing from my stool to grab another beer. "You won't get fired. If nobody saw you hit him don't worry about it. He's not going to go to management and tell them he'd been sleeping with one of his physical therapist assistants and when he finally told her that he was married she hit him. The question is, do you want to continue to work there?"

"It's such a good job, and they work with my school schedule, but I don't know if I can stand to see him every day. I guess I'll start looking for a new job and see how it goes. I can't afford to quit if I don't have another job lined up, and a part of me doesn't want him to win."

"Then don't, he's the asshole not you," Alex said and we toasted in agreement.

Ten

Blood and Baristas

The crowd was thick as we made our way up the stairs to the main floor of the venue. A large octagon cage came into view over the heads of the bystanders. It was fight night, the only thing better than sex and mint chocolate chip ice cream. There was just something about watching half naked men beat the shit out of each other. It was like something primal inside awakened at the sight of blood and sweat, it was hot as hell.

Surprisingly enough, despite her sweet and innocent appearance, Evie was all about the bloodlust. She never missed a fight if she could help it. The girl went nuts when the fighters got in the cage, out screaming everyone and yelling about take downs and arm bars. The commentary she provided was almost more entertaining than the actual fight. She couldn't help it though; it was in her blood. Her father ran a Jiu Jitsu gym that trained a lot of the fighters so she had a vested interest.

Evie was an only child, and since her mother passed away when she was little she practically grew up in that gym. The girl was a total badass but you would never know it. On the exterior, she was all sunshine and rainbows but if you crossed her she would beat you senseless without breaking a sweat. I'd only seen her in action outside of the gym once. We were in college and some guy at a party got handsy. She laid him out so quick if I hadn't been standing right next to her I wouldn't have caught it.

"Let's grab a beer before we find our seats," I called out to the group. Everyone nodded and we made our way over to the bar. The line was stupid long and we had to wait ten minutes to even get up to the counter. Once we had drinks in hand we made our way over to the reserved seating area. Knox and I were standing in the aisle waiting for everyone to file in and take their seats. I liked to be on the outside since my bladder was the size of a fucking lima bean when I drank beer and I would inevitably have to pee every five minutes. Just as Knox was making his way into the row a guy bumped me from the side, causing my entire beer to spill down my front.

"Shit, motherfucker!" I yelled as the icy drink soaked my shirt.

"Oh, fuck! I'm so sorry!" The guy said hurriedly and began to pat at my chest with his sweatshirt.

I stood stock still as he continued to try and sop up the mess he'd made. Was this guy for real? He didn't even seem to notice he was practically groping me.

"The fuck?" Knox said from behind me. The guy froze and looked up at me suddenly realizing where his hands were.

"Shit, sorry!"

I laughed at his embarrassment. He was pretty cute, tall, kind of geeky in a hipster sort of way. "Don't worry about it, if there's a wet t-shirt contest later I'll be prepared."

"And you'll definitely win," he said quietly, then realizing he'd spoken the words aloud his eyes got huge. He looked up over my shoulder where I was sure Knox was looming. "Sorry dude, I didn't mean any disrespect. Really, I was just paying your girl a complement." The excuse was lame but he seemed flustered so I let it slide.

"Oh, no! He's not my boyfriend," I said quickly.

"Why you gotta say it like that?" Knox questioned, coming out from behind me.

"Why you gotta be such a cockblock?" I replied, through gritted teeth, equally annoyed.

"Really, I'm so sorry. I'll pay for dry cleaning or whatever."

Turning back to the klutzy guy I smiled, "Tell you what, you buy me another beer and we'll call it even. Yeah?"

"Absolutely," he said quickly, looking relieved.

"Lead the way."

We snaked through the crowed and came to a stop at the tremendous line.

"So what's your name?" he asked.

"Briar, yours?"

"Pete." There was a moment of silence before he continued, albeit awkwardly. "So, what do you do for a living?"

"I work in customer service. What about you?"

"I'm a barista," he said with a little too much enthusiasm for a man in his late twenties.

"Cool," I literally had nothing to say in response.

"Yeah it's a great job, I love it."

Nothing, dead fucking air. I blinked up at him, willing him to continue the conversation because I had absofuckinglutely no clue where to go from that.

"Do you like coffee?" he asked.

Is this real life? Where are the hidden cameras?

"Sure, just as much as the next person I guess."

"I love coffee. We roast our own beans at the shop I work at. Not like one of those chain shops. Coffee really is an art; you have to be really careful not to burn the beans or over froth the milk. When it's done right you can pick up on all the flavors, my favorite is this dark roast we make. You can taste the currants and smell the rich tones."

What in the actual fuck?

The corduroys and Vans should have tipped me off, dammit. The line moved at a snail's pace as Pete continued to regale me with the tales of his career. Finally, we reached the bar and Pete ordered our beers. Just when I thought it couldn't get any worse, it did.

"Oh hey, there's my buddy. I lost him in the crowd right before I bumped into you. I came with some friends; this really isn't my scene."

No, really?

An image of Pete sitting on a spotlighted stage playing the bongos came to mind.

Pete's voice pulled me out of my daydream. "Yo, Reid. Over here!" he shouted and waived his hand over his head. My body froze, it couldn't be. I slowly turned around to see that it indeed was. Supermarket Reid, aka tried-to-run-me-over Reid, was making his way toward us.

His brow furrowed in confusion for a moment when he saw us but I could tell the second he recognized me because a slow grin tugged on the corner of his mouth.

Pete slung an arm over me when Reid got close, "Hey, man. This is—"

"Briar, I thought we agreed it was best to end things. Trying to get in with my friends really is beneath you."

I glowered at him and shrugged off Pete's arm. "Hey asshat, run over any innocent women lately?"

"Whoa, you guys know each other?" Pete asked, sounding somewhat disappointed.

"Oh, yes. We had a torrid love affair in aisle ten," Reid answered.

"And then he tried to kill me."

"Um, what?" Pete asked, more than a little confused.

"Nothing," Reid and I said in unison, which earned him another glare from me.

Turning around I grabbed my beer from the bar. "Thanks for the beer Pete, I've got to get back to my friends," I said and booked it back to my seat.

"Whoa, do I need to kick somebody's ass?" Knox asked as I dropped into my seat.

"No it's fine."

"You sure about that? You seem pretty pissed."

"I'm sure, drop it. They're announcing the first fight."

I sat stewing for the next hour. I did not scan the crowd for a flash of red hair. Nope, not once. Okay maybe once, twice tops, but I didn't see him so it didn't count. Where had he gone? Not that I cared. Why did I let that bastard get under my skin? And why the fuck was he here. This did not seem like the place a guy like Reid would go willingly. Not that I really knew him, but still.

When the fight was over, we reconvened on the sidewalk outside of the venue. There were people milling around everywhere while our little group checked their phones and discussed what to do next. I wasn't paying attention. I was also not looking for Reid again. When I saw him our eyes locked and that stupid fucking grin tipped the corners of his mouth again. Why did I find that sexy? I broke our gaze and tried to pay attention to the conversation happening in front of me while still keeping the sexy ginger in my peripherals.

"I'm starving," Evie said.

"I don't care where we go as long as they have a bathroom. I've got to piss like a racehorse," Alex complained.

"The Red Dragon?" Knox offered.

"No strip clubs tonight," Evie whined. She hated them with a passion. For somebody with a vagina she really did not like the sight of them.

"Jesus, it was just a suggestion!" Knox raised his hands in surrender.

"Let's just hit up Jackie-O's, they serve breakfast all night," Kellen offered. He was always the peacemaker.

"Sounds good to me. I can get those hash browns with gravy," Alex agreed.

"Eww! You're fucking gross," I said, finally joining in on the conversation.

"But you love me anyways," she said batting her eyes at me. I finally understood what Reid had meant in the store the other day. Because that shit didn't work for Alex either.

Suddenly I heard my name being called out from a not so far distance.

Shit, fuck, motherfucking cocksucker!

He was not coming over here. I snapped my head in the direction of the voice and sure enough Reid was sauntering up to us. I narrowed my eyes and made the very best bitch face I could muster, but his gait didn't falter.

"Hey, you going to introduce me to your friends?" he asked as he sidled up to me.

"Fuck off."

"Ah, come on now. Just because we ended things doesn't mean we can't be friends."

"Go piss up a rope, you tried to kill me."

"Pfft, that's ancient history. Besides, it was an accident. I would never intentionally run over my chocolate crossed lover, you know me better than that."

"Chocolate, what?" Evie asked. Four pairs of eyes had been ping ponging between Reid and I during our exchange.

"Sorry, it's an inside joke. Briar and I were almost soul mates until fudge covered Oreos drove a wedge between us. It's tragic really," he said shaking his head. "I'm Reid by the way."

"Hi, Reid. I'm Evie, and this is Alex, Kellen and Knox," she replied, ever the little hostess. "How exactly do you know Briar?"

"It's a beautiful story, do you want to tell them, or should I?" He asked turning to me. I could feel my face start to burn as my friends looked on in amusement.

"I actually don't know you at all, and I'd prefer to keep it that way." I didn't really know why I was being such a bitch. He didn't really mean any harm, but I was still pissed about the brushoff. If he wasn't interested, then why come over here?

"Now, we both know that's not true. Otherwise you wouldn't have come here to find me."

I lost it. This guy was unfucking believable. "I did NOT come here to find you. I go to every one of these fights and I have never seen you here before. If anything, it's more likely you had your friend bump into me as an excuse to talk to me again." I didn't hold back any of the sass this time, letting it all hang out.

"Nah, not my style. I knew that if I ran into you again then it would be a sign that we could get past our chocolate differences. No, my dear Briar. This is fate."

I blinked. This guy was insane, straight out of the goddamn looney bin. "Are you fucking crazy? Like, off your fucking meds crazy?"

"Crazy in love maybe."

I looked around at my friends for help but they were all stifling their laughter and in no hurry to come to my aide. "You have got to be fucking kidding me right now."

"You can't fight fate. The Gods have spoken; you have to go out with me know. It's your destiny."

At that my friends erupted in laughter. Traitorous bastards, every last one of them.

"Oh my God, this one's a keeper. Briar where the hell did you find this guy? And why the fuck have we not heard about him?" Alex asked.

"What?" Reid exclaimed in mock horror, "You didn't share our tale of love and loss?"

"Jesus fucking Christ." This guy was not going to let it go.

"We're going to grab a bite. Why don't you join us and you can tell us all about it," Evie offered.

"I'd love to," Reid said at the same time I shouted, "No!"

This of course caused another round of hysterics and Alex exclaimed that she was going to piss herself if we didn't get to a bathroom soon.

Reluctantly, I followed the group the short distance to the restaurant with Reid keeping step with me. I couldn't exactly stop him from following us. Even though I didn't want to admit it, a small part of me liked the fact that he was being so persistent. Despite the fact that it was mostly in jest.

When we were seated at a long table in the center of the small restaurant, Reid at my side of course, he slipped his arm around my shoulder. I immediately shrugged it off and stared at my menu. The rest of the group was milling over their own menus and carrying on normal after-fight conversation, discussing their favorite K.O. of the night. Even if I'd wanted to participate I couldn't, my brain had been so full of Reid that I couldn't focus on the fights and I had no clue what they were talking about.

Reid leaned in close and whispered in my ear, his warm breath causing a shiver to run down my spine. "In all seriousness, I really would like to get to know you. And I'm sorry for almost running you over, it was a complete accident."

I glared at him from the corner of my eye, "If you wanted to get to know me so bad then why did you book it at the grocery store?"

He sighed, "What I said before was true, I figured if I was meant to get to know you then I'd eventually run into you again. It's kind of the way I operate. There are signs everywhere you just have to look for them."

"So you really are crazy."

He chuckled lightly, "Not crazy, I just believe that the universe works in mysterious ways. I have faith that things will happen the way they're supposed to."

"Whatever." I really didn't have anything intelligent to say in response. This guy was an enigma. Although I would never admit it, his philosophy on life kind of intrigued me.

"Give me a chance, just one chance. You know you want to."

"You don't know me at all, how could you possibly know what I want?"

"Can't you feel it? I can. There's a connection here, I told you we can't fight fate."

I stared at him for a long moment. Our foreheads bent together, nearly touching. I could smell the beer on his breath as it slowly warmed my lips. He was so close. I could see every freckle that decorated his face. He wasn't covered in them but he had his fair share. His eyelashes were light brown and insanely long, I was instantly jealous. Why was it that men always had awesome eyelashes and we were stuck with stubby little bristles? His eyes were the lightest green I'd ever seen, like a fresh leaf or a new flower bud. Or like pond scum.

"All I can feel is hunger. And a sense that you are completely in-fucking-sane."

He laughed, "I'll wear you down eventually."

"Whatever," I said and turned my attention back to my menu.

Eleven

Ginger Love

My phone chirped on the floor next to the bed. I groaned and rolled over to blindly reach for it. Cracking my eyes open, I glanced at the offending device and quickly slammed them shut again.

Fuck! Why is looking into your phone when you first wake up like staring into the goddamn sun?

I dared another glance after a minute of nursing my scorched irises. It was a text message. From a number I didn't recognize. I opened it thinking it was one of those promotional messages from one of the million solicitors Knox had signed me up for over the years. I had to constantly screen my calls otherwise I was likely to go insane with the constant stream telemarketers offering me a fucking timeshare if I'd just sit through one short presentation at no cost. Needless to say, I'd gotten pretty handy with the 'block number' feature on my phone over the years.

But when I pulled up the text it wasn't a promotional blast message, instead, it contained two words.

Unknown: Dinner tonight?
Me: Who is this?
Unknown: Reid. Is that a yes?

What in the actual fuck?

Me: How did you get my number?

I'd completely ignored him for the rest of the night after his little declaration. I certainly didn't give him my number, so how? Unless someone else did.

"Evie," I growled. My suspicions were confirmed when his next message came through.

Reid: A little birdy told me.

Son of a bitch! "Evelyn Marie!" I screamed as I struggled to kick my legs free of the tangled sheets. Finally freeing myself, I stumbled across the room and into the hallway, hollering the entire time. "You nosey little cunt!"

"What the fuck are you prattling on about, you whore?" Evie's sleepy voice called out as her head popped up over the back of the couch where she'd been sleeping.

"Why are you sleeping on the couch?" I was momentarily side tracked.

"You were fucking snoring so loud I thought you were operating heavy machinery in your sleep. I could hear it all the way across the damn hall and through a closed door. You really should get that shit checked out."

"Shut your filthy mouth! I do not snore."

"Oh we are so not getting into this. What time is it anyways?"

"Seven."

"Ugh, why are you up so fucking early on a Sunday?" she complained.

"I didn't get the luxury of sleeping in because *somebody* gave dickhead Reid my phone number and he decided to text me at the butt crack of dawn!"

"Ah, shit."

"Yeah, so if I don't get to sleep, neither do you," I said, walking around the couch and sitting directly on her.

"Fuck! Get off of me." She struggled and squirmed trying to dislodge her legs from under my ass.

"Why would you give him my number? I was pretty clear what with all the 'Fuck off', 'don't talk to me', and 'eat shit and die' that I was throwing at him all night, was I not?"

"Oh please, we all know that was for show. You like him, it's pretty obvious."

"No. No it is not obvious, because I don't fucking like him. He's a prick!"

"Why?"

I looked at her blankly, "Huh?"

"Why is he a prick? Explain why you can't stand him. Convince me, and I'll back off."

"He tried to kill me!"

"Enough with the fucking melodrama. He was backing up his truck. He stopped, didn't he?"

"Only after I screamed at him!"

"So he didn't see you, and maybe you didn't see him. It's not like it would be completely out of character for you to not be paying attention."

"Whatever. He drives a spray-painted truck!"

"Spray painted how?" Alex asked as she entered the room from the hallway.

"I didn't know you were up," I said.

"Well I sure as hell wasn't going to get any sleep with you two screaming."

"Sorry," I mumbled.

"No worries, I need to be a part of this conversation too. Start at the beginning," she said sitting on the other side of Evie who had finally gotten free from me and was sitting cross-legged on the center of the couch.

"Well, this no good—" I was cut off by Evie.

"It's too fucking early for your long-winded ass. I gave Reid her number last night and he texted her this morning. Now she is trying to convince me he's a prick."

"Got it, go on. You were saying something about a spray-painted truck?" Alex asked.

I rolled my eyes, "I am so not as dramatic as you both make me out to be," I said glaring at them.

"Jesus Christ, this is going to take longer than I thought, I'm making coffee," Alex responded and Evie and I trailed behind her into the kitchen.

"Like I was saying," I began, glaring at each of them in turn before I continued. "His truck is spray painted. Not just rattle canned flat black, it looks like a fucking freeway overpass."

"Like street art?" Alex interjected.

"Yeah, I guess. I don't know anything about that stuff but there are a bunch of weird pictures all over it."

"Huh, that's pretty cool actually. Was the tagging any good?" Alex asked, her brow furrowed as she focused on scooping out the perfect amount of coffee grounds. She even leveled out each scoop with the back of a knife, like precise measurements were required to make a basic cup of coffee. She took OCD to a whole new level.

"How the hell am I supposed to know? Besides, I didn't get a good look since my life was flashing before my eyes."

"It makes sense." Evie pipped up.

"How? He's a grown man driving around in a tagged up hooptie!" I exclaimed.

Evie shared a look with Alex before she replied. Her words slow and drawn out as if she was speaking to a child, "Because he's an artist?" her quirked brow and squinty eye told me she thought I might not have all of my mental faculties about me.

"How do you know that?" I demanded. Not that I cared, because I didn't. If she wanted him she could have him. Hell, I didn't even like the guy.

So why are you about two seconds away from going full blown bitch mode on your best friend? And why is she still looking at me like that?

"He told us last night," she replied, still using that condescending tone.

"When?" I was lost. I hadn't even been drunk last night. Instead I spent the majority of the night obsessing over the fact that douchebag McGee was getting under my skin. I didn't even remember most of what happened at the restaurant. In fact, after Reid had rolled up his sleeves when our food was served I hadn't heard much of anything. The two times I'd seen him before he'd been wearing a hooding and slightly baggy jeans so I hadn't been able to tell what he was working with. When he'd revealed those tattooed forearms, corded with muscle and just the right number of veins I had lost all sense of hearing. Forearms were my weakness. There was just something so fucking sexy about a nice set of arms, and full sleeve tattoos were like icing on my hot man cake.

"When we were grilling him. What the fuck, Briar? Did you space out for the entire night?"

"Apparently," Alex said, giving me a knowing look. She knew more than anyone my obsession with ink. One of the few things I had been conscious of from the night before was Alex and Reid discussing tattoos.

"So what else did you find out?" I asked.

"He works at a local brewery," she started, ticking off fingers as she went on. "He's 28 years old, single, and he plays the guitar."

"Oh my God it's worse than I thought!" I exclaimed.

"What the hell is wrong now? Those are all awesome qualities. A hot artist, musician, and free beer? It's like smoldering, sensitive bad boy 101," Alex said.

"Really? Because this is what I see, he's an artist, and artists are sensitive." I made a gaging noise and continued ticking off my own list, "Musicians are moody, he's 28 and still drives around in a spray-painted vehicle, he's a *ginger*," I made sure to emphasize that point, "and last but certainly not least, he's a total hipster. Not my type, thank you very much."

"You forgot to mention the beer."

"Oh big deal! So, he can get us free beer. I bet we have to listen to his pretentious ass bitch about the finer points of craft brew. It's the coffee guy from last night but with alcohol. I bet he complains about the beer selection wherever he goes too, what a little bitch."

"You have got to be kidding me with this shit. Stop stereotyping," Alex scolded. "At any point in the two times you've met him did he sound moody or sensitive? The guy is hilarious and he can give as good as he gets. You just don't like that he gives you a run for your money in the wit department. Also, shut the fuck up about the ginger thing, you know you like it. You've had ginger fever ever since the third Harry Potter movie."

I gasped in mock shock, "How dare you."

"Oh shove it," Alex said.

"You can't fool us," Evie piped up, "don't forget, I caught you masturbating to Harry Potter junior year."

"I was high!" I shouted. "You can't hold sober me responsible for what high me did, it's not fair." In my defense, I had been smoking all day, and it was Deathly Hallows Part I. Anyone that tells you Ron wasn't hot in that one is lying and they can go choke on a dick.

"Dude, how did I not know about this? For real Briar, Ronald Weasley gets you all hot and bothered?" Alex asked, positively giddy over this new piece of blackmail material, I'm sure.

"That is so *not* the point. This guy is the antithesis of my type. I don't do soft and feely, I do strong and stoic. Wham bam, thank you ma'am. None of this 'tell me what you're thinking', 'let me write you a song' bullshit. I go for the caveman, not the poet." I stated, loudly.

"You're right, he isn't your type," Alex agreed. I was about to start nodding when she continued. "But your type hasn't really worked out for you, has it?" I hated her, I loved her, but I also really, really, hated her.

"Briar, sweetie, you need to stop self-sabotaging. This guy was made for you, and he is obviously interested. Give him a chance, he might surprise you." Evie coaxed.

"You both suck ass," I mumbled and took a sip of the coffee Alex had just handed me. They were right, of course. Reid didn't seem like a he had any creepy fetishes and he had the ability to carry on a conversation, which was more than I could say about the last few dates I'd been on.

He actually seemed kind of awesome, but I wasn't about to admit that out loud. I had to admit, if only to myself, that he was pretty hot despite the fact that he was the polar opposite of my normal type. He was quick witted and fun. I hadn't ever met a man that could banter back and forth with me like that, not without some prompting at least. There was something about the ease of our conversation in the grocery store that had stuck with me. If I was going to be honest with myself, I think that was what hurt me the most when he walked away. It was as if he hadn't just felt what I had, and that made me feel way too vulnerable for my liking.

I had issues, big fat Dr. Freud issues. Commitment freaked me the fuck out, and even the mention of marriage had me breaking out in hives. It wasn't that I didn't want to get married and have kids eventually, that had always been the plan for the future. The very distant future. As in, when I was forty and had it all figured out. I knew someday I wanted to settle down, the problem was that in order to do that I would need to trust someone. And trusting a man other than my brother or on occasion, Knox, was just not in my comfort zone. My stomach churned at the thought of having to depend on someone else for anything, let alone half of a mortgage and help raising kids.

Unlike most crazy people I was completely aware of the fact that I was crazy. I had daddy issues, and I, like so many other women, was insecure. I knew it. The problem was, I couldn't get over it. I dated men that wouldn't leave me, men that I was never going to be invested in because I knew they weren't the one. I always ended relationships before anyone could get too close, before I had a chance to get hurt. Because if I was the one calling the shots then it was easy to pretend I didn't care. The difference now was that I actually wanted to change that about myself. I wanted to let myself fall, but the fear of landing was paralyzing.

"But you know we're right. Just respond and see what happens. Worst case scenario, you go out with him and realize he really isn't a match,"

Evie said kindly. She was the trusting one of our little trio. A quality that more times than not left her with a broken heart and tears in her eyes.

"And best case scenario, you hit it off and end up fucking like rabbits," Alex added with a smirk over her coffee cup. I grabbed the closest thing to me, a pen, and flung it at her head.

"Ugh! Fine, but let the record show that I'm doing this under duress."

Twelve

Beer and Bacon Bowls

He was late. It was five past seven, the scheduled meeting time, and I was sitting in a bar by myself. Looking like a fucking idiot. *Strike one,* I thought as I glanced towards the front doors for the third time in as many minutes. I had vetoed the dinner offer, instead opting for drinks, less pressure and a shorter time commitment.

I swear to God if this guy stands me up after chasing after me the way he did, I am going to hunt him down and make him earmuffs out of his own ball sack.

Just as the daydream began to get good I heard the stool next to me scrape across the battered wooden floor. Unlike most dive bars the place he'd chosen didn't have carpet or linoleum. Instead it boasted a rustic feel with an old wood bar top and old school wooden stools.

"Hey, sorry I'm late," Reid said in way of greeting.

I glared at him in return and sipped my beer. I could see from the corner of my eye that he was wearing a button-down shirt with the sleeves rolled up.

Don't look at his arms, don't look at his arms, shit I totally looked at his arms. Damn, why does he have to have good arms?

"Okay, yeah I deserve that. I don't believe in excuses so I'm just going to apologize and hopefully we can move on?" He posed it as a question, and when I didn't respond he nodded and got up from his stool. I had a moment of panic that he was going to leave me there, but then he did something so much worse. He got down on his knees beside my stool. I turned my body to face him and gave him my best what-the-fuck-are-you-doing look, it didn't work.

"Briar Rose Jameson," He announced loudly, staring up at me from his position on the floor. "I am deeply troubled and guilt-ridden for causing you any undue distress by my tardiness for this, our first union which holds such promise for what I hope is our impending bond. Please take this expression of regret and find it in your tender heart to absolve me of my indelicacy."

I was flabbergasted, my mouth was hanging open and I could feel my eyes bugging out of my head. He was still there, on his knees at my feet, in front of an entire bar of people who I knew

109

were staring at us, because it was deadly quiet all around us.

Think Briar, shit, I have to say something.

He was just staring at me, hands together as if he were praying.

"Uh, yeah. You're forgiven?" I stumbled out, it was more of a question than a statement. The bar erupted in cheers and Reid beamed at me as he returned to his stool as if nothing had happened. "What the fuck was that?" I asked in horror. I was still in shock by his absolute disregard for social formalities.

He just shrugged, "An apology."

"Do you always apologize like that?"

"Only when I really mean it," He said and then winked, and signaled for the bartender. The dude actually winked at me, who is this guy?

"Right," I said dubiously and checked for the closest exit. With my luck, he was going to be asking me if his napkin smelled like chloroform any minute.

The bartender came over with a pint of the same beer I was drinking and set it in front of Reid, he thanked the bartender and turned to me. "Do you like the beer?" he asked throwing me off my train of thought.

"Ah, yeah actually. It's really good."

"Thank you," he said with a smirk.

I looked from the beer to him several times, "You made this?"

"Yup," Reid pointed to the sign above the bar that read 'Bearded Jack's Tap House'.

"So you work here?"

He nodded, "I make beer, it's an awesome job."

"I've never been here before, how long has it been around?" I asked, curious because despite the mentally unstable company, the beer was on point.

"A few years, I've been here since the beginning. It's a smallish operation. Big enough to stock the tap house and a few local pubs. We get a lot of neighborhood traffic since we fill growlers too."

"Cool." Jesus, could I be more lame? I always sucked at this part of a date, it was as if I went completely brain dead, my responses consisting of repeating 'awesome' and 'cool' over and over again. I was such an idiot, I was just staring at him, not talking like a dumbass.

Reid gave me a half smile and slipped off his stool, "Come on, bring your beer. I want to show you something."

I followed him behind the bar, but stopped short when he started to push through a door that led God knows where. "Wait, where are we going?" I asked suspiciously.

He laughed, "Calm down, I'm going to give you a tour. You'll like it, I promise."

"Fine, but if you try to pull anything, I'm not afraid to bludgeon you to death with this pint glass."

"Noted, now let me show you how beer is made," he grinned at me and grabbed my free hand, pulling me through the door. We hurried through the stock room and kitchen with Reid shouting hellos at everyone we came across and me giggling behind him. He threw open a door at the back of the kitchen and I followed him through to a dimly lit hallway.

We passed a room with huge bay windows that looked like a cross between a laboratory and a lunch room. I tugged on his hand, signaling him to stop. "Hey, what's this?" I asked breathless.

Reid came to stand next to me, not letting go of the hold he had on my hand, "This is where we taste the beer before it gets bottled. It's also our break room," he laughed. "There's not a lot of extra space since most of the warehouse is used for actually brewing the beer."

"What did this place used to be?"

"It was a carpet warehouse, actually. We converted the showroom into the tap house and revamped the front of the building. Essentially, the rest was just an open concrete box once we took out the pallet racks. We got the right permits, brought in the equipment and voila."

"That's pretty amazing, how long did it take?"

"About seven months, give or take. Come on, there's way more to show you than the break room," he said over his shoulder as he continued to pull me along down the hallway.

The sound of machinery got louder the farther down the hall we went, with one last turn we came to a set of yellow swinging plastic doors that read 'Authorized Personnel Only'. "Hey, are you sure it's okay for me to be back here? I don't want to get you in trouble."

He chuckled and shook his head like him getting in trouble was the most ridiculous thing he'd ever heard. "Relax, Briar. You worry too much."

"Just because you don't have a care in the world…" I trailed off when he tugged on my arm, pulling me towards him until we were standing face to face.

His hand slipped from mine and he trailed it up my arm softly, his fingertips lightly grazing the exposed skin. His hand continued north and brushed a piece of hair behind my ear. He leaned in and I swear to God he was going to kiss me, and I wanted him to.

"I care about a lot of things, Briar," he whispered, so close to my lips I could practically taste his words, "I just don't let worrying about them get in the way of living life." He pulled away, grabbing my hand once again, and led me into the warehouse.

What the fuck just happened? No, seriously. What in the actual fuck?

I was contemplating seven different ways to kill him as I scrambled to keep up with his long strides and not spill my half empty beer. I couldn't believe I was still holding onto the glass. Jesus, my hand was starting to cramp.

Reid spent the next half hour taking me through the warehouse and explaining the different stages of brewing. Who knew it was such a process? He prattled on about mash mixers, extracting sugars, and hops ratios. I tried to keep up, I really did. Beer was something he was obviously passionate about. I was always complaining how men never listened, I didn't want to be hypocritical but somewhere around the time he was explaining the filtration process, I tuned out.

It really wasn't my fault, he was gesturing with his hands, his beer since forgotten on a bench somewhere. Those arms, they were going to be the death of me. I found myself staring at the way his muscles moved beneath his white button down, if the frontal view was a distraction, the view from the back nearly made me lose consciousness.

He was standing in front of me, explaining C02 blow off from yeast fermentation or some shit, and all I could do was pan up and down his body. I was like a fucking dog in heat. How had I gone from mean mugging to wanting to jump his bones in less than an hour? The way the muscles in his back

114

moved and caused his shirt to stretch and strain, and dat ass. Damn.

"The temperature and aging time is determined by the type of beer we're making. Briar?"

I jerked my head up to his face. I had been staring at his ass while he was talking, but he'd turned around when he said my name causing my line of sight to be right at dick level.

"Uh, yeah that's really neat," I stuttered.

Neat? Did I just get transported back to 1955? Get it together bitch, do you want this guy to fuck you or give you his fucking letterman jacket?

"It's kind of ironic that it takes so much math and science to make a beverage that's primary function is to make people stupid," I said.

Smooth, insult his livelihood, much better.

Reid threw his head back and barked out a laugh, "You don't hold any punches, do you?"

"Not typically, no."

"Well you're right, there is a lot of big brain stuff involved in making the simple man's drink of choice."

"Shit, I didn't mean to offend you. I really do think it's interesting— "

"So interesting that you weren't paying attention?" He asked, quirking an eyebrow.

I couldn't tell if he was joking or not so I went for honesty. Which usually in my case was not the best policy, but it was all I had at this point. "It's not my fault if your ass was more interesting than yeast fermentation. It's a compliment. In fact, you should be thanking me."

Reid's smile was huge, "I was totally fucking with you, but thank you," he said with a bow. "I tend to get caught up when I'm explaining what I do and I don't realize that other people don't share the same passion."

"Oh I have a passion for beer, just not making it. Mostly my enthusiasm is expressed using a funnel of some sort."

He looked down at the floor, hiding his smile, and shook his head. I got that look a lot. But then he glanced back up at me and cocked his head to the side in the most adorable way. Next he blew my mind by saying the three little words that every woman secretly prays to hear from a man on the first date, "Are you hungry?"

***

"But it has peanut butter on it, with bacon," I said, my face contorted in the most unattractive of ways.

Reid chuckled at my obvious disgust, "Don't be so closed minded. Trust me, it's the best thing you'll ever put in your mouth."

I gave him a coy smile, "I seriously doubt that."

"Jesus!" He tilted his head to the sky and muttered something I didn't catch under his breath. When he finally looked at me again I noticed his face was flushed.

"Are you blushing?" I jibed, surprised that Mr. Cool could be so easily flustered.

"No, maybe a little bit. You're different," he said, shooting me an inquisitive look, as if he was trying to figure me out. "I never know what you're going to say next."

"Yeah, I get that a lot. I wasn't born with much of a filter, if it pops in my head, nine times out of ten it's going to come out of my mouth."

"I like that. I always know where I stand with you, not many women are like that."

Danger Will Robinson, danger! Alarm bells were going off in my head, we were diving way below the surface here and I was not equipped. "So are you actually going to make me eat a burger with peanut butter on it? What if I was allergic?" I blurted out.

"Are you?" He asked, seeming to pick up on my need for a change of subject.

"No, but it just sounds so fucking gross. What's next? Shrimp and blue cheese?"

"They actually have that too," he laughed. "Look, if you don't like it I'll buy you something different but you have to at least try it. Come to the dark side, we have delicious food."

"Regret this I hope I won't," I mumbled under my breath and stepped towards the food truck.

Reid stopped me with a hand on my shoulder, "Did you just Yoda me?"

"Mmm hmm, I did. It's the lack of filter thing, I quote movies too so get used to it."

He blinked a few times, and ushered me to the line. After we ordered our food Reid led me over to a tent that was set up with picnic tables and portable heaters before running back to pick up our food.

I scooched closer to the heater and rubbed my arms, it was surprisingly cool for late August in Portland. I glanced around the tent at the other food cart patrons and I had to admit it was a pretty awesome idea for a date. Not that I would tell Reid that, we were still thoroughly entrenched in the ball busting stage, I couldn't show weakness by letting him off easy.

"Are you ready for a taste bud experience for the ages?" Reid asked, as he placed our food on the table.

"You're confident, you may want to dial it down a notch or two."

"I'm pretty sure you're going to like it."

"I'm pretty sure I won't."

He picked up a French fry and threw it at my face, "Stop being a negative Nancy and eat your food, I slaved all day for that."

I snorted, "I cannot believe you just threw a fry at me!"

"Stop stalling, eat."

I glared at him and reluctantly unwrapped my burger. If you could even call it that. With a grimace, I took a minute to steel my nerves before taking a tentative bite. Reid was looking at me expectantly but I didn't let my face give away anything as I chewed. I slowly placed the burger down in the basket and wiped my mouth with a napkin. All with excruciatingly slow precision to torture him.

"It's alright," I announced, taking a sip of my beer.

"Bullshit."

"Excuse me?"

"I call bullshit, you love it, you just don't want to admit that I was right."

"Whatever," I rolled my eyes and took another bite of my burger. It was one of the best burgers I'd ever had but there was no way I was going to tell him that.

"Ah ha! That's enough confirmation, my work here is done."

"Shut up and eat."

We spent the next half hour talking and enjoying our food. He told me more about working at the brewery and volunteering at the youth center. I told him about getting canned, I opted to leave out the one-night stand drama going for the PG version, and moving into the house with my girls. When we were finished, Reid took my hand again and we walked back to the brewery. I'd had more fun than I ever thought I would with him. It had been so long since I'd had a good date I didn't want it to end.

We reached the tap house and Reid glanced down at his watch.

Here comes the brush off.

And here I thought we'd been having a good time.

"It's not that late, do you want to do something else?" He asked, completely surprising me.

"Sure, what did you have in mind?"

He gave me a boyish grin and grabbed my hand again, tugging me down the street once again, "I've got an idea, I think you'll like it but it's a surprise."

"If you tell me you've got a website to show me, I'm out."

"What?" He asked over his shoulder as he dragged me along behind him.

"Never mind."

He brought us to a stop in front of the infamous spray painted truck. Opening the passenger side door, he bowed, "Your chariot awaits, my lady."

"Oh my God, you are such a dork!" I exclaimed, climbing into the surprisingly clean cab.

"Thank you," he said, giving me a wink as he slammed the door with enough force to shake the entire vehicle. "Sorry," he called out, "the door tends not to shut all the way so I have to really slam it."

"That's what she said," I mumbled to myself as he rounded the hood and settled into the driver seat.

The sounds of *Linger* by The Cranberries blasted through the speakers as soon as he cranked the engine. He scrambled to turn it down, but the damage was done.

"What? Why?" I asked, trying to catch my breath, I was nearly hyperventilating with how hard I was laughing.

He hung his head in shame, "Alright, get it out now because we are never speaking of this again."

"Fat chance, this is blackmail material," I wheezed.

"Oh come on! 90s pop is uplifting, and name one person you know that doesn't like The Cranberries."

"Not the point, just because everyone likes them doesn't make it any less embarrassing for you to have them turned up to 11 in your car."

"You know what? That's fine, I'm comfortable enough in my masculinity to own it," he said nodding his head. Then he rolled down his window, stuck his head out of the car and screamed at the top of his lungs, "I FUCKING LOVE THE CRANBERRIES AND I'M NOT AFRAID TO ADMIT IT!"

"Oh my God! Stop it!" I shouted as I attempted to pull him back into the cab by his shirt.

When he was done, he fell back into his seat, laughing just as hard as I was. We sat in the cab for what felt like forever trying to catch our breath, but as soon as I thought I'd gotten myself under control we made eye contact and it started all over again.

Once we settled down, Reid pulled out onto the road. I still had no idea where we were going but I didn't feel any unease. Aside from the awkward conversation after his epic apology, it had been the easiest date I'd ever been on. I didn't feel the need to watch what I said or act a certain way. I always felt like I was 'on' during a first date, like it was a fucking audition or something.

There were so many rules for a woman when it came to dating. Don't be too aggressive, don't swear, laugh at his jokes, mind your manners, and only eat fucking salad. It's not like I actually did any of that before, but I was still careful what parts of my personality I put out there. Because really, if you let all your crazy hang out at once there's no mystery left. But as we sat there chatting about everything and nothing, all at the same time I realized that Reid made me feel comfortable being myself, which was something I was so not ready to process. I wasn't even supposed to like him.

"I gotta ask, what's up with the spray paint?"

"Ah, I guess I should've know that was coming. It's kind of a long story…"

"I've got time."

"Well, when I was a teenager I thought I was hot shit. I'd sneak out and go around town tagging any blank surface I could find. Eventually I got caught."

"You got arrested?"

"I didn't get booked or anything, they just wrote me a ticket and took me home. I had to go before a judge though. Luckily she was pretty cool and just sentenced me to six months of hard community service."

"Did you have to paint over your tags?"

"Yeah, that was part of it too. I ended up serving my time working at the community youth center in my home town, ironically I was teaching art. After my time was up I just kept coming back and when I moved here I started volunteering at the center in Sellwood. I guess you could say I started using my powers for good instead of evil."

"Someone thinks highly of themselves," I laughed.

"But really, I was an idiot. I thought I was sticking it to the man but after a couple of months working with the kids I realized I was going about it the wrong way. 'You have to be the change you wish to see in the world.'"

"Did you just quote Gandhi?"

"Yes, yes I did. It's true though. I like the work I do with the kids at the center, I help them channel their creativity in a positive way, one that won't get them arrested."

"That still doesn't explain the truck."

"It was a project I had them work on. They were bored with the mediums they had to work with so I let them have at my car."

"Whoa, kids did this? That is so cool!"

"Yeah I know, there's this one kid, Emma, she's seventeen and one of the best raw talents I've ever seen. She did the whole hood and when I showed a buddy of mine her stuff he actually hired her to paint a mural in his pizza shop. She has a really shitty home life and no matter how much I told her how good she was; she still didn't believe it. But God, you should have seen how she lit up when I told her about the mural. It was like she finally believed she could be more than her circumstances.

"I'm trying to work with her on her other subjects because she's failing nearly every class other than art but she doesn't believe in herself and I have no idea how to convince her. She's smart, like so smart. She has all this potential just locked away in that head of hers, the only problem is that no one has ever taken the time to show her what she can do. A lot of artists struggle with math and science, it's just the way their brain works, but I don't think that's her problem. I think she's just been told so many times that she's not good enough and not worth the effort that she's just accepted it as a fact.

"I don't know how I'm going to do it, but come hell or high water I'm going to make her see how special she is. I was talking with Alex the other night and she mentioned she still had some friends over at the Art Institute. I was going to try to take her on a tour or something, have her talk to some of the students there and get an idea for what it's like. You know?" He asked as we pulled into a parking lot.

I didn't even know where we were because tears were streaming down my face and all I could see was a watery version of Reid illuminated by the glow of the streetlight. My eyes hadn't moved from him the entire time he'd been talking. He was so animated when he was talking about the kids and especially Emma. I could tell how much he cared, and it broke my heart and made it swell at the same time. "You're kind of amazing, you know that?" I croaked.

He let out a breath and scratched the back of his head, "Nah, I just want to help."

"And that's the best part, you have no idea," I shook my head and dried my eyes. Pulling down the visor I wiped the mascara from beneath my eyes and smoothed out my hair, slowly pulling myself back together. I glanced out the window to see where we are, "You brought me to a 24hr Walmart?" And just like that the heavy mood was lifted.

***

"What about this, you know you need one of these," I said thrusting the contraption at his face.

"What the hell is this?"

"It's a donut maker, duh! You put the batter in here and then press this and the perfect amount drops into the oil in the perfect donut shape," I responded in my best infomercial voice.

"Whoa, that's scary. Exactly how much Home Shopping Network do you watch?"

"It's not my fault. Evie used to have gnarly insomnia in college and she'd stay up all night watching infomercials." We'd rummaged through the clearance shelves, discount movie bin, and had moved on to perusing the small 'As Seen on T.V' section.

"I see, well I'm not much of a donut maker but I'm sure I could find a use for this," he said picking up another item. "It's a bacon bowl maker? Wait, it said you're supposed to put it in the microwave, who cooks bacon in the microwave?"

Doubling over, I laughed so hard that I had to take a knee. Gasping for air I choked out, "I...totally...have...one!" before succumbing to another round of giggles.

"No way, I don't think I can see you anymore. I looked the other way with the white chocolate but microwaving bacon is against my religion."

Finally catching my breath, I moved to stand up, "It was a white elephant gift. I've never actually used it so you're safe to keep seeing me."

"Oh thank God, it would have been such a shame. I mean who else was I going to wander around Walmart with at eleven on a Wednesday night?"

"True, not many women are as cool as me."

"That's an understatement," he said smiling down at me. He smiled a lot, and I realized I smiled a lot when I was with him. Yet another thing to stow away and dissect at a later date.

"So what's next?" I asked.

"To the toy aisle! We have bikes to ride and hula hoops to hula" he announced and I followed his lead by marching behind him the entire way across the store.

***

When we finally got back to the brewery where my car was parked it was midnight and I'd literally laughed a stich into my side.

"You did not!" I protested.

"Yes, I did! I told you I was an idiot!"

"But you actually put icy hot on your ball sack? Why?"

"I lost a bet!"

"I can't believe that," I said, shaking my head.

"Oh there's video evidence somewhere, my buddy Ryan taped the whole thing."

"I have to see that! You have to get it!" I sat up in my seat and leaned over to him, shaking his shoulder for emphasis.

"I'll see what I can do. Where did you park?"

"Around the back," I said, climbing out of the truck. I was sure to slam the door so it closed properly. Reid came around to my side and took my hand, walking in the direction of where I had parked. "You don't have to walk me to my car."

He turned his head and gave me a what-the-fuck look, "Uh yeah I do. It's midnight and we aren't in the best neighborhood, I'm not going to let you walk to your car alone. What kind of a jackass do you think I am?"

I smiled and shoulder bumped him, "Thank you."

"For what?"

"For an awesome night, I don't think I've ever laughed so much on a date before."

"Whoa, wait. This was a date?" He asked a tinge of panic in his voice.

Did I misjudge this entire night?

I whipped my head up, how the fu—His smile clued me into the fact that he was totally fucking with me. "You are such a prick!"

"You should have seen your face! It was like a cartoon, your eyes bugged out of your head!"

I slapped him in the chest with my free hand, "What the fuck is wrong with you?"

128

"Oh come on, you've been flipping me shit since we met. Are you trying to tell me you can dish it but you can't take it?"

"Whatever!"

"I like it when you say whatever, it means I won."

"Ugh, wha—shut the fuck up."

Reid laughed for the hundredth time that night and released my hand. I felt kind of sad because I'd gotten used to the feel of my hand in his, but then he put his arm around my shoulders, bringing me in close to his body and suddenly I was no longer the least bit sad. Funny how that works. I wrapped my arm around his back as we walked the rest of the way.

When we'd reached my car, I turned to face him, my back against the drivers' side door. Before I could get a word out he reached up and took my head in both hands. His fingers sifted through my hair and his thumbs rested on my cheeks.

"I had a great time tonight," he whispered, "I'd really like to see you again."

I was far too gone in Briar's fantasy wonderland to speak so I just nodded. He gave me that sexy half smile I saw in the bar and leaned down to kiss...my forehead.

What in the motherfucking fuckity fuck fuck?!

My brain couldn't even process what had just happened. "Drive safe, text me when you get home okay?" I nodded again, and unlocked my car.

Going through the motions of getting in, starting the engine and driving away all the while wondering what kind of douche canoe has the most amazing and unique date ever and then doesn't kiss the girl.

He waved as I pulled out onto the main road and I didn't even have the mental capacity to respond. A million scenarios flew through my head on the drive home. Maybe he was Mormon, or gay, it wouldn't be the first time that had happened to me. What if he'd taken a vow of celibacy and didn't want to be tempted by my Scarlet Johansen lips? Yeah fucking right, in my Real Housewives collagen dreams maybe. What if the date didn't really go as well as I thought it had? No, he specifically said he wanted to see me again. Oh, my ever-loving God, what if I had stank breath? I quickly blew into my hand and tried to sniff it to see if I could smell my own breath. I couldn't. Fuck! How? How did this happen? There was only one way to find out. I hit number two on speed dial and turned on the Bluetooth.

"Yo, what's up?" Alex's voice came through the speakers.

"Are you home?"

"Yup, just got here. My last appointment ran long."

"Good, is Evie there?"

"Yeah, what the fu—Oh! Your date with Reid was tonight, how'd it go?"

"I'm ten minutes out, grab the tequila, it's going to be a long night."

"Shi— "

I disconnected the call before she had a chance to respond. She knew the protocol. I needed to debrief them and then together we would we would pick apart the entire date and put it back together, finding out what the fuck went wrong.

Thirteen

Twat Ticklers and Texts

"Come smell my breath!" I screamed as I flew into the house.

"What the fu—" Evie started, but I cut her off when I lunged and breathed in her face.

"Smell my breath! Does it stink?" I asked in desperation.

"What? No! It kinda smells like beer but it doesn't stink."

I stood there staring at her, my blood heated as my anger started to bubble over.

"Whoa, whoa, whoa! Alex, get your ass in her, Briar's about to blow a gasket!" As soon as the words left her mouth Alex slid into the living room on her socks *Risky Business* style, with a pint of Ben and Jerry's in hand.

Thinking about that scene in *Risky Business* made me think about the white button down Reid

132

had been wearing earlier and I blew like old faithful. "THAT MOTHERFUCKING, COCK SUCKER, SHIT STAIN, DICK CHEESE EATING, TWAT TICKLING, SON OF A CUM GUZZLING CUNT!" I screamed while repeatedly hitting the couch cushions with my purse.

"Did she just say twat tickling?"

"Shut the fuck up!" I bellowed, I wasn't even sure who'd asked the question. Yes, I had said twat tickling, and no I didn't know why.

Alex walked over to me and shoved the ice cream under my nose, "Here, you need this more than I do right now."

"Thanks," I said, as I flopped on the couch and attempted to regulate my breathing.

Who knew beating the shit out of your couch could be such a workout?

"So... it went well?" Evie asked hopefully.

I gave her my best I-want-you-to-die-a-thousand-fiery-deaths glare and shoveled a giant spoonful of Phish Food into my mouth.

"Why don't you start at the beginning and tell us what happened?" Alex asked softly, which indicated I'd been acting certifiably bat-shit crazy, because Alex was never the gentle one of our little trio. I closed my eyes and let the chocolaty marshmallow goodness calm me. When I felt sufficiently medicated I disclosed every detail of the five-hour date.

When I'd finished an hour later, they were both just as confused as I was.

"So wait, let's recap, shall we? He was late, which sucked, but then he made up for it with a public Pride and Prejudice-esque groveling. He took you on a tour of the brewery that made one of the best beers you'd ever tasted. Got you to break out of your shell by eating totally weird but delicious food. Made you cry by telling you about his volunteer work and his passion to help disadvantaged children. Took you to Walmart to basically goof around and act like a kid again. Walked you to your car and told you how much fun he'd had and how he couldn't wait to see you again. Then, after what has been described as the single best date in the history of dates, he kisses you on the forehead. Did I miss anything?" Evie asked.

"Nope, that's the gist," I mumbled into the empty ice cream carton.

"Hmm," Alex squinted at me, "maybe, now I'm definitely not an expert at this dating shit, but maybe he actually likes you. Don't look at me like that!" she scolded. "What I mean is maybe he was nervous and didn't want to screw it up by going too fast. Not every guy is a horn dog that wants to jump straight in the sack. Maybe, just maybe… gasp… he wants a *relationship*."

"Fuck you, twat!" I yelled and threw my spoon at her. She ducked my projectile and cracked up laughing.

"Seriously? So, what, he didn't end the date with you horizontal. I know you aren't used to it but some guys are actually decent human beings."

134

"But he didn't even kiss me! He gave me the blow off kiss, I mean come on who kisses someone on the goddamn forehead?"

"You, my friend, need to dial the crazy bitch down about 20 fucking notches," Alex demanded with a stern, don't-fuck-with-this-Latina-ass-because-I-will-make-you-wish-you-were-never-born look.

"Fine, but let the record show, I'm still pissed. First, he blew me off at the grocery store, then he chased me, conned my friends into giving him my number, and pestered me until I went out with him. Then, he gave me the total brush off, AGAIN! I mean, there's only so much a girl can take before she starts getting a damn complex." Just as I finished my final rant, my phone pinged in my purse. Pulling it out, I saw I had two missed texts from Reid. "What the fuck?"

"What is it?" Evie asked.

"Reid text me."

"What did he say?" Evie squealed, and I was suddenly sandwiched between the two of them before I could even pull up my messages.

Reid: Hey, just wanted to make sure you got home okay.

Reid: I know this is really uncool and if you tell anyone I probably won't deny it but please don't tell anyone for the sake of my man card okay? I had a really great time with you tonight, like more fun than I think I've ever had. You're beautiful, adventurous, kind, witty, and most of all intelligent.

135

You make me laugh more than anyone I've ever met. I hope you'll continue to let me get to know you because I have a hundred more adventures I'd like to experience with you. But for now, goodnight, funny girl.

"Hot damn!" Evie screamed, bouncing up and down on the couch next to me.

"Yeah, even I've got to admit that was on point," Alex agreed.

"He didn't say I was sexy, what does that mean?" I questioned, and as soon as the words left my mouth, four pillows flew directly at my face. "Shit! Okay, yeah it was pretty romantic, I'll give him that."

"Girl, you better text him back. Did he actually text you to see if you got home alright? Yeah he's a keeper." Alex said.

"Well, I was kind of supposed to text him when I got home, he asked me to right before I left."

"Oh my God, and he still sent you that text after you blew him off? You lucky bitch!" Evie shouted.

"Ugh, yeah so maybe I overreacted a bit." I admitted sheepishly. I re-read his text and did a little of that internal swooning I'd done when we first met. I quickly typed out a message while the girls were talking amongst themselves. I'd always shared everything with them, but after the text he sent it didn't feel the same.

Me: Yes, I'm home safe and sound. The girls had to get details as soon as I walked in the door. Sorry if I made you worry. Tonight, was amazing, thank you for a date I'll never forget. Goodnight for now

I don't know why, but I suddenly had this urge to keep this part private. What happened tonight felt different than anything I'd ever experienced. I was still pissed that he didn't kiss me, but I was also a little bit gooey in the center with all the feels from his follow up text. Which scared the tits off me, but I kind of wanted to see what happened more than I was scared.

"I'm going to bed," I announced as a hefted myself from the couch.

"Hey, you didn't even break into the tequila!" Alex called after me.

"Don't need it, I'm just going to crash. See you in the morning," I waved over my shoulder on my way down the hall and I swore I could hear the what-the-fuck look they gave each other.

Fourteen

Weapons-grade Douchebag

"What a condescending, pretentious, limp dick, tuna twat!" I screamed, emphasizing each insult with a slap to my steering wheel.

It was the first day of my new temp job, and it was only noon. The call center job had been a six-week assignment. When I was placed at Briza & Associates for a two-month temp to hire position I had been thrilled. Finally, a job that didn't require reading a script and allowed me to get up from my desk more than lunch, two ten minute breaks, and two more closely monitored bathroom breaks. It may sound so bad, but that's because you don't realize how much you get up from your desk throughout the day until you're not allowed to.

It was supposed to be a simple secretary position, a two-month assignment with the potential to be hired on full time. At this point, I wasn't sure I would last two days, let alone two months. Mr. Briza, or Mr. Briza-lite as I liked to call him since the guy I was working for wasn't the same Mr. Briza whose name was on the building. Instead I was blessed to work for his weapons-grade douchebag of a son. Less than four hours into my new job and I had already plotted thirty-six ways to murder my new boss and make it look like an accident. Honestly, if the government was monitoring my google history I'd have already been brought in for questioning.

Sometimes in life you meet a person and you can instantly tell they're a special kind of asshole. If you happen to come across this person in your work life, you find a way to maintain your professionalism and deal with them. I'd had to deal with such people numerous times in my professional career, for Christ sake, my previous boss was the closest thing to the devil on earth that I could imagine. However, this spoiled, self-important, sewer sucking slime ball was far and beyond anything that I'd ever encountered.

I'd arrived five minutes early this morning, but that didn't seem to matter, as soon as the receptionist walked me through the office door to show me to my new desk the cocksucker reared his overly greased head.

"Hi, you must be Mr. Briza. My na—" I started to introduce myself but he cut be off.

"Of course I'm Mr. Briza, did you not see the plaque on the door when you walked in? Jesus, are the dispatchers at the agency competing to see who can send me the most incompetent temp?" he barked. Immediately my hackles were up.

Who the fuck does this little ass dragon think he is?

I quickly remembered how much I needed this job. It paid significantly more than the call center position and I'd worked for horrible people before, I could handle this guy. I stayed silent for a moment with my head held high in an effort to let him know I wasn't afraid of him. He was a small man, which was probably why he overcompensated with the dickhead attitude. His black hair was slicked back with so much product he was a gold chain and loud shirt away from being a used car salesman. I kept my composure as his harsh black eyes scanned me from head to toe. An asshole I could handle but if this guy turned out to be a pervert I would hightail it back to the unemployment line.

"My name is Briar," I said finally, done with letting him leer at me. "The receptionist has already given me the passcodes and I have my basic job description. Do you have a list of duties I can get started on for you?"

"You can start by getting me a coffee. Venti, triple, half sweet, non-fat, caramel macchiato at 120 degrees."

"I'm sorry?" I knew it made me sound like a twit, but I was so caught off guard, did he really want me to go down the street and order him *that*?

"Did I stutter? Go, now!"

Oh, hell no. I walked over to my new desk and set my things down, his beady eyes following my every move. I calmly picked up the pad of paper that lay on the desk and a pen, finally turning to him.

"Can you please repeat that?"

He huffed out a sigh and then spoke, his words slow and dripping with condescension, "Venti, triple, half sweet, non-fat, caramel macchiato at 120 degrees. Think you can manage that?"

Maybe he was testing me to see how far he could push me before I broke, whatever he tried, it wouldn't work, this bitch had bills to pay. I smiled sweetly, "Absolutely, I'll be right back."

The rest of the morning went much the same, until I retreated to my car for my lunch hour and my day went from bad to worse. My phone rang as I was pulling out of the deli parking lot where I'd just picked up my lunch. I reached into my purse to silence the damn thing when, *crunch.*

The car had come to a violent and abrupt stop.

Fuck.

The first thing I saw when I looked up was a shiny BMW emblem. Double fuck. The silver car pulled forward onto the shoulder of the road and I followed. Letting out a litany of curses under my breath, I searched the glove box for my insurance card. I had enough half empty water bottles in my car to sustain a family of four during a drought but I couldn't find my fucking insurance card? Another minute and several choice words later I had my insurance information and ID in hand as I stepped out of the car to meet the unfortunate driver that I'd smashed into.

The guy was nice enough, and after examining the damages (a dented license plate for me and a scratched bumper that would probably cost more than my entire car to fix for him) we exchanged information and went on our respective ways. Thank God I still had full coverage insurance because there was no way I had the cash to replace the bumper on a fucking BMW, I wasn't even sure if I had the cash to cover my deductible.

Once I got back to the office I pulled out my phone to identify the dildo that caused my accident. No I wasn't going to admit it was my fault for irresponsibly taking my eyes off the road. My day had been absolute shit and I deserved to blame someone else for this. At least for a little while.

Checking my phone, I saw three missed calls from the last person on earth I wanted to talk to.

My father.

Of course, today of all days he would decide to reach out to me for the first time in nearly five years. The fucker.

I deleted the messages he'd left and blocked his phone number. A small sense of satisfaction followed by a huge wave of guilt washed over me. I couldn't stand my dad, but I didn't hate him. Acknowledging that I still cared about what happened to him didn't negate the fact that I was still hurt that he'd ruined our family. I unblocked the number but I wasn't going to call him back. If it was important he'd call Kellen and he would relay the message.

Glancing at the clock in my dashboard I noticed my lunch was almost over, so much for the sandwich I'd picked up. It was just as well; the events of the last hour had spoiled my appetite.

***

The rest of the week went much the same as my first day. Mr. Bitchy pants as I'd taken to calling him in my head, continued to treat me like a derelict and bark orders at me like I was a fucking dog. I, in turn, kept my attitude in check and my mouth shut.

The job itself wasn't all that hard. It mostly involved organizing his inbox, taking messages and updating his calendar. Occasionally, I would venture down the hall to make copies or collate something. All in all, it was a pretty cushy job. I guess the extra pay was just to deal with the asshole boss.

Actually, by Friday afternoon I was feeling pretty good. I still mentally murdered my new boss roughly six times an hour, but I'd figured out a system to keep the barking at bay. I'd stop to get his special-order coffee before work each day and hand it to him first thing when I walked in so he didn't have a chance to start snapping.

Way to go the extra mile, huh? I took pride in my work, despite the fact that I was way overeducated to be a coffee goffer, I would do whatever job I had to fullest extent of my ability. It also helped that I spit in his precious coffee every morning before I got out of my car, you couldn't be perfect all the time, right?

Fifteen

The Cowboy and The Librarian

"Where are we going?" I questioned as Reid started to drive out of my neighborhood.

After a week of talking on the phone every night I decided he wasn't a creeper and agreed to let him pick me up for our second date. Surprises seemed to be his thing, because after nearly two solid days of begging he still hadn't given up what we were doing on our date.

I normally hated surprises. I was the kid that would spend hours painstakingly peeling the tape off of all of my Christmas presents under the tree to figure out what I was getting before Christmas morning.

While it was killing me not knowing, it was also kind of exciting. I'd never met a guy that stuck to his guns the way Reid did. The men I'd dated in the past gave it up somewhere between the sixth and tenth time I asked, but Reid was immune to my pestering. I liked that he wasn't a pushover, it was good for someone with a personality like mine. If a guy let me bulldoze him, I tended to get bored rather quickly. That was my problem with most of my previous relationships, at least the ones that stuck around long enough to claw their way out of fuck buddy status and into full blown monogamy.

"You'll find out soon enough," he responded with a teasing lilt to his voice.

"Whatever."

"I love it when you say that," Reid laughed.

"It doesn't mean what you think it means. You don't win just because I stop fighting."

"Uh, yeah I do. It's called a surrender."

"Uh, no. It's a cease fire. I'm not waiving any white flags over here, buddy."

"Whatever you need to tell yourself, babe."

I tried and failed miserably to hide the smile that took over my face at hearing him call me babe. He'd said it a few times during our late-night phone conversations but it felt more intimate now in person for some reason.

The sound of Reid's blinker pulled me out of my butterfly induced fog and I leaned forward to look out his window so I could see where we were going. My eyebrows creased with confusion when I saw the familiar blue and white sign.

"First Walmart, now Goodwill? I'm sensing a theme here," I said, not trying to hide the surprise in my voice. I wasn't upset or disappointed, if anything I was intrigued. I knew I was going to have fun no matter what Reid came up with, and I'd probably end up laughing my ass off by the end of the night.

"Did you learn nothing from our last date? Dating is about getting to know someone, it doesn't matter how much money you spend, it's about the quality of the time. When you take someone out to a fancy dinner you learn the same boring things, and no one is really themselves. You end up acting like this cardboard version of yourself, so worried about which fork you use, you forget why you're really there. Throw two people together with nothing but a department store as entertainment and you see who they really are. Fun is what you make of it, and I'm pretty sure you and I could have fun doing just about anything."

I smiled at him sweetly, "I wouldn't speak so soon, you haven't met my family."

Reid tossed his head back and laughed, "I'll take that under advisement. Now come on." We hopped out of the car and as soon as Reid rounded the hood to my side he took my hand in his.

You know how sometimes when you hold hands with someone it can be the most awkward experience of your life? Your hands start sweating and shaking, and you can tell the other person is either just as uncomfortable or totally grossed out by your excessive sweating? Yeah, none of that happened when Reid held my hand. It felt natural, he wasn't too tall so it didn't feel like I was holding on to my dad's hand, and while he did make me nervous. It was the good kind, not the profusely sweaty kind.

"Okay, so you know how you were telling me the other day how you were kind of overwhelmed with everything?" Reid asked as he led me over to the women's section of the store.

"Yeah," I answered. "What about it?" I remember the exact conversation he was talking about.

I'd had a particularly shitty day at work and as soon as I came home the girls started laying into me about how I was acting different and asking me about a million questions. I had locked myself in my room and called Reid because suddenly he was the only person in the world I wanted to talk to. I'd told him how I was feeling. How I'd always been the wild child; people never really knew what I was going to do or say next. How I felt like because of my personality I always had to be on, like I couldn't have a bad day and just want to be quiet because it wasn't 'normal' for me.

"You said you wished sometimes you could just be someone different. Right?"

"Uh, yeah."

"I want you to pick out an outfit, whatever you want. The only requirement is it has to be something you would never normally wear. You're going to come up with a whole new name and personality. I'm going to do the same thing. Then we're going to go on our date, but we have to stay in character all night, deal?"

I blinked at him, was he nuts? "You're insane."

"Probably, but you're going to play along anyways so really, what does that say about you?"

"Touché."

"The last catch, you only have twenty dollars so spend it wisely," he said handing me a crisp twenty-dollar bill.

"You don't have to pay— "

"Shut up. This is my idea, these are my rules, take the money and go. I'll meet you outside in a half hour," he said, shoving the money in my hand and taking off towards the men's section.

Shrugging, I turned towards the vast sea of racks that made up the women's section. Wandering through the aisles, I contemplated my alter ego.

I was on my third rack of clothes and still had no idea who I wanted to be for the night when inspiration hit me in the form of the ugliest sweater I'd ever seen. The crew neck sweater had a giant picture of two cats floating in a galaxy background, complete with multicolored constellations. The thing made me dizzy just looking at it, it was perfect. I paired the sweater with acid washed, high waisted jeans circa 1989 and clear jelly sandals. There was something about the plastic smell that brought me back to my childhood. To top it off I grabbed an oversized bow clip from the accessories section and headed to the checkout line.

While I waited to pay for my items I scanned the store for any sign of Reid but I couldn't see him anywhere. Looking at my phone I noticed I only had five more minutes left of my allotted half hour to get changed and meet Reid outside. Twenty dollars and one very confused checker later I had my new identity in hand as I made a beeline to the bathroom to change.

I almost didn't recognize Reid when I walked out of the store. He was leaning against the building, one leg bent with his booted foot resting on the wall behind him and his head was tilted down underneath a huge white cowboy hat.

"Oh my God!" I couldn't hold in my laughter as I took stock of his outfit, a red and white checkered pearl snap button shirt and jeans with black cowboy boots. He even had a bolo tie.

Pushing off the building he surveyed the look I'd put together, one side of his mouth kicking up in a half smile. "Well, hello there, little lady," he said in a terrible southern accent. "My name's Billy Joe but my friends call me Bubba, and you are?"

I had to take a minute to control my breathing before I answered, "Very nice to meet you Bubba, my name is Mildred. I don't have any friends, so you can call me Mildred."

Reid coughed to cover up his laugh and tipped his hat at me, "My pleasure, Ms. Mildred. How abouts you and me get some grub?"

"That sounds delightful." I took his proffered arm and let him lead me to the truck.

***

I slipped up a few times during dinner, falling back into my own personality. Reid quickly squashed it, insisting we continue with our little game. At first it seemed completely ridiculous, which it was, but after a while the whole experience was actually kind of freeing. It was strangely refreshing to pretend to be someone else entirely. There was no recourse, I could do or say whatever I wanted and it wasn't me, it was Mildred. Each story we told was more outlandish than the last, and by the end of dinner we were laughing our asses off. Much to the dismay of the wait staff and other patrons of the restaurant.

I learned that Bubba came from a long line of dairy farmers and always dreamed of moving to the south to be a real cowboy. Mildred was a librarian who enjoyed smutty romance novels and talking to her nine cats.

After dinner Reid took me home and even went as far as to walk me to the door.

"Ma'am," He said, tipping his hat as we reached the door. "Thank you for sharin' a meal with me. I have to say; it was a pleasure."

"Well, Bubba, I had a delightful time. Thank you for a wonderful evening," I responded.

I tried, I really tried to keep a straight face but it was impossible with the 'awe shucks' look he was giving me at the moment. I snorted, loudly, then burst out in embarrassed giggles, covering my face with my hands, because snorting was truly the absolute least sexy thing I could do.

Once I'd regained my composure I peeked at him through my fingers, "I'm sorry, can we stop now?"

"Yeah, I think the experiment has run its course."

"Thank you for tonight, Reid. Honestly, it was exactly what I needed."

"No problem, but I should be thanking you for playing along. I know it sounded crazy but I just wanted to try and get you to forget the shit for even just a few hours," he shrugged.

"It worked," I nodded, staring up at him.

He smiled and pulled his hat off with one hand as the other drew me closer to him. I was so focused on his eyes as he stared at me and continued to move forward that I almost didn't hear the sound of his hat dropping to the porch. His other hand came up and cupped around the back of my neck, his thumb caressing my jaw.

Slowly, without taking his eyes off of mine until the last possible second, his mouth descended on mine. His lips were soft and warm against my own, and the kiss built from soft to firm. When his

152

tongue swept out to touch my upper lip I groaned, granting him the access he needed. Reid controlled the kiss, his tongue slipping inside with teasing flicks. My whole body started to heat and I was totally ready to take this thing to the next level because if he could kiss that well, there was no telling what other talents he might have. I was prepared to discover each and every one.

Reid pulled back and swiped a thumb across my lower lip. "Mmm," he said dipping his head and sneaking another kiss. "I've been wanting to do that since I met you in the cookie aisle."

I took a deep breath, trying to regulate my breathing and working up the courage to ask him in.

Jesus Christ Briar, just fucking do it. It's not like you've never invited a guy back to your place after a date.

Yeah, but I'd never asked a guy that I wasn't sure would say yes. Not to mention none of those guys were Reid.

Fuck it, I'm just going to do it.

"Do you want to come in?" I whispered, nodding my head towards the door, as if he needed a visual. God, I was an idiot, I hadn't even meant to whisper it'd just come out like that, all breathy and desperate.

I'm such a chicken shit.

Reid smiled and squeezed my hand, "As much as I'd like to, I think it's best if I say goodbye now."

153

"Oh, umm, yeah okay," I stammered and tried not to feel like total shit.

Yeah no dice.

"Hey, don't do that," he said, pulling me tight against his chest once more. "I just want to get to know you more before we go there, not saying that's what you had in mind— "

"Oh I did," I interrupted, finding my voice again. "You are totally saying no to sex right now."

Reid let out a heavy sigh and rested his forehead on mine. I was pretty sure he mumbled 'fuck me' but I let it go.

"Briar, I really like you. I want to do this the right way. I don't want to rush it and miss the opportunity to really get to know who you are. I've done that and it hasn't worked out for me in the past. You deserve to have someone woo you."

I snorted, "Woo? Who says that? I don't need to be wooed."

"I didn't say you needed it, I said you deserved it. You're worth putting in the time."

And there go my panties.

His words soothed the sting of rejection a bit, but not enough to keep the sarcasm at bay, "You're right. If we have sex now, you'll get addicted and we'll never talk again because all you'll want to do is bang."

Reid chuckled, "You have no idea."

That statement had me all sorts of tingly but I pushed through the lust and volleyed back,

"Having a magic pussy is a blessing and a curse, but that's my burden to bear."

"Jesus, can you please not say shit like that?"

"I thought you liked how I was, now you want me to watch the profanity? You can't have it both ways bucko." I teased, watching the blush rise from his neck.

"No, I just... never mind" he pinched his eyes closed and shook his head.

I knew what he meant but I liked fucking with him, I'd noticed that he blushed whenever I said something overtly sexual, it was kind of cute.

"Good night," he said leaning in for another kiss, this one sweeter than the last.

"Good night, text me when you get home?" I asked.

A slow grin spread across his face, "Yeah, no problem."

I watched as he walked back to his truck, but always the gentleman, he didn't drive off until I was inside the house and I knew this because I was staring through the window like a fucking tweaker.

"What the fuck?" I heard Alex exclaim behind me.

Whipping around, I came face to face with both of my best friends. Evie had a giant bowl of popcorn with a handful mid-shovel into her mouth as she stared at me, unmoving. At first I thought they were wondering why I was staring out the window, but then I remembered what I was wearing. I couldn't contain the bark of laughter that burst out of my mouth.

After explaining why I'd left the house in a cute maxi skirt and I came back looking like an 80s cat lady, I told them what happened on the porch, hoping they'd be able to lend some insight.

"That's sweet!" Evie said as she chomped on her popcorn. For a woman in the health industry she ate like a 300-pound linebacker and drank more beer than a frat boy.

"As much as it pains me to admit it, I agree with Evie. This guy sounds legit," Alex said earning a smack from Evie.

"I guess, it's just weird. We can talk about anything and everything over the phone, have two fantastic dates and all I get is a few kisses. Maybe he's gay? Oh, my fuck, what if he's a virgin? I can't sleep with a fucking virgin! I have never slept with a virgin!"

"Calm the fuck down, you crazy bitch. I doubt he's a virgin, or gay. From what I've seen and heard from you, he just sounds like he's trying to take it slow." Alex reasoned.

"But why? I don't understand. What's his angle?"

"Umm, hello? It's romantic. He wants to get to know you as a person and develop a relationship with you before you get physical. That's like romance 101." Evie chimed in.

"Oh sweet mother of all that is holy. He has a tiny penis. That's it, it has to be. He's trying to lure me in so when he shows me his little popcorn shrimp I'm less inclined to dump him."

"STOP!" Alex shouted, "I'm only going to say this once so listen up buttercup because it's time for some real talk. You are the queen of the surface relationship. You like having a boyfriend as long as it's not too serious because you're afraid to let anyone in. As soon as shit starts getting too deep you jump ship so you can't get hurt. You're freaking out about Reid because he's heading for deeper water and you don't know how to navigate."

"I'm going to stop you right there; can we get off this boat analogy?"

"Fine, you're afraid of letting him in because you might get hurt. He's starting where your relationships usually end and he's being upfront about it so you can't justify a reason to get out because there isn't one. You're a grown ass woman. You like this guy, so stop being afraid and just go with it, because if you don't you'll regret it."

"When did you become the relationship expert?"

"I'm not. I just know what it's like to regret not giving someone a chance." I wanted to ask her what the fuck this regret talk was about but she turned around and left the room, shouting over her shoulder, "Stop being a pussy."

I turned to Evie, "Do you know what that was all about?"

She shook her head, "No, but she'll tell us when she's ready. She's right you know; it sucks to hear it but it doesn't make it any less true."

"Okay fine, but if he has a pencil dick I'm going to be pissed," I said, leaving Evie in the living room eating popcorn and flipping through Netflix.

My phone chimed as soon as I got into my bedroom.

Reid: I'm home. Goodnight, funny girl.

Me: Thanks for getting me out of my head for a while. Goodnight.

I crawled into bed and thought about what Alex had said. She was right. I was terrified of trusting someone enough to let them in, because if they left they might take a piece of me with them that I could never get back. I'd seen how love could destroy someone and I didn't ever want to feel like that, but I had to consider that if I always played it safe I'd never get the good part either. I'd never been in love, but I knew I wanted it. I just had to figure out if I was willing to risk my heart to get it.

Pushing the heavy thoughts from my mind I replayed my night in my head. Reid really was something different. No one had ever listened to one of my rants and actually heard what I was saying, but he did. He realized what I needed and he found a way to give it to me. Unconventional as it may be, it was really sweet.

Cat sweater: $5.99, mom jeans: $7.99, jelly sandals: $4.99, bow clip: $.99, best second date ever: priceless.

Sixteen

Hairballs and Hissy Fits

"Hey, big brother! Have I told you how much I love you lately?" I said as soon as Kellen picked up the phone.

"What do you need?" he grumbled. Shit, I must've woken him up. I instantly felt like shit since I knew he was probably sleeping off the 24-hour shift he'd just had at the fire house.

"Well, I'm kind of having a captain save-a-ho moment," I winced. My brother is good to me. Always bailing me out of weird situations so I could only imagine what was going through his head at the moment.

"What did you do? Am I going to need bail money?" He asked.

"What? God, no. The drain in the tub is clogged and I don't know how to fix it. Well, I kind of tried to fix it but I don't think it worked," I made sure to add just the right amount of whine to my voice. Since I'd never really had a serious boyfriend all the man shit I needed done around the house usually fell on Kellen. I tried not to bug him too often but given the state of my tub after I'd tried using a chemical drain cleaner, I didn't have a choice. I had no idea what I'd done wrong but the chemicals didn't go down the drain and I was pretty sure they eating through the tub.

"Fuck! How many times have I told you not to try and do this shit on your own? Do you remember the time you tried to change out the florescent bulb in your kitchen?" he asked.

I remembered the incident in question well. I had accidently broken the bulb when I was trying to take it out of the light fixture. How was I supposed to know you had to twist then pull? Did you know that when a florescent light bulb breaks it practically blows the fuck up? Well, it does. I had to wear an eye patch for two weeks because I got tiny shards of glass in my eye.

"Ugh, not likely to forget Knox calling me a dirty rotten pirate hooker for a month. I just didn't want to bother you, I'm sorry. But could you hurry because the chemical smell in here is starting to make me woozy."

"Go in the other room! What the hell is wrong with you? Jesus, I'll be there in ten."

***

"Have you talked to dad?" Kellen asked as he pushed the snake down the clogged drain. Of course, he would bring up that twat. I loved my brother, I did, but he could be a pushy asshole sometimes.

"No, the answer has been no every time you've asked for the past five years and it will still be no for the next five years."

"Come on, you can't stay mad at him forever."

"Yes I can. He broke mom's heart," I bit out.

Kellen grunted as he hit a difficult spot with the snake, "Briar, be fair. They got divorced years ago. Lots of people get divorced, it doesn't mean you can just shut out one of your parents for the rest of your life."

"Why not? He shut out mom," I was well aware that it wasn't the same thing but I still felt like it was a valid enough point to bring up.

"That's different, you're his kid. He's still our father no matter how much you don't want him to be."

"How are you not mad at him Kellen?" I asked, confused.

Kellen sighed and sat back on his heels, turning his head to look at me, "Because, he's still our dad. He's still the guy that taught us to ride a bike and built us a treehouse in the backyard. He's still the guy that had Star Wars marathons with us in our blanket forts. You can't just erase all the good stuff just because of one shitty situation. You don't have to understand why he left mom to have a relationship with him, or at the very least have a conversation."

"How do you wake up and just decide that you've fallen out of love with your wife after 25 years of marriage?" I asked, but I really meant how do you wake up 25 years later and decide your family isn't enough for you.

"It's not that I'm not angry with the situation, Briar. I don't like what happened, but I'm not going to punish him for the rest of my life over a choice he made for himself. We have to move on."

That was the difference between me and my brother. He'd always been a roll with the punches kind a guy. He was resilient. I was not. I held grudges, big time.

The problem was that I just couldn't wrap my head around the fact that my dad abandoned my mother. It wasn't like he was cheating, and from what I could tell he wasn't having a midlife crisis. There were no toupee's, no sports cars or big spending. He simply sat us down during Christmas five years ago and told us that he'd fallen out of love. It was a bullshit excuse if you asked me.

I never wanted to get that close to anyone. Not when there was a chance that the other person would wake up one morning and decide that your love wasn't enough.

"He wants to come to Thanksgiving," Kellen said with a hopeful look in his eyes.

"Absolutely not," I automatically blurted out, "Mom's coming for Thanksgiving and I am not going to put her in that position." I was shaking my head emphatically by the time I'd finished the sentence. Kellen huffed and I could see his jaw clench. I knew he was frustrated, but so was I.

"I already talked to mom she said she was fine with it. She's moving on with her life, it's time for us to get over it," he said turning back to the task at hand.

"I can't believe you asked mom! Of course, she's going to say it's okay, she's not going to tell you no."

"Briar, seriously she seemed fine with it," he grunted as he started to pull up on the snake.

"I'll be the judge of that. I'll call her and ask her, but I swear to God Kellen, even a hint of her being uncomfortable and the answer is no."

"That's fine," he said, standing up and turning to me. "But I'll tell you what's not fine. This." He held up the glob of hair that he'd pulled from the drain and I started to dry heave.

Seventeen

Eat a Fucking Cheeseburger

Reid led me through the volunteer center to a back room that housed their art studio. I was amazed when we walked through the door and a room full of kids' faces lit up. It was like walking into the room on the arm of a movie star. He was clearly adored.

As if on cue, a group of girls in the far corner called out in unison, "Hey Mr. Reid," they giggled.

Reid tipped his head in their direction, "Ladies," he said in way of greeting.

"Yo, Mr. Reid," a pimple faced kid hurried over to us. More like hobbled, since his pants were sagging so far down his legs they actually hindered his ability to walk. When he finally made it over to us Reid gave the kid an elaborate handshake and a pat on the back.

"Hey Doug, how's it going?" Reid asked

when they pulled apart from their man hug.

"Yo man, how many times I got to tell you to call me Dougie fresh?"

"Sorry, Dougie fresh, I must've forgotten," Reid said with the barest hint of a smile.

"Whoa, whoa, whoa, wait a minute there," he said as he caught sight of me standing slightly behind Reid. "Oh damn, who's the honey?" I feel the need to mention that 'Dougie fresh' was as white as a sheet of paper, probably weighed a buck ten soaking wet and was wearing a hat that was about three sizes too big for his head.

"Douglas, her name is Briar," Reid said in authoritative tone that made all my lady bits take notice. Down girl, I mentally reprimanded myself.

Now is not a time to lead with the vagina. There are children present.

"I apologize, ma'am," he said to me. I nodded back and gave him a smile to let him know that I wasn't offended. Reid sure had these kids whipped into shape. "You gotta see this fresh tag I just did," he said, bouncing with excitement.

"On a canvas?" Reid asked with a raised brow.

"Yeah, man. You know my Ma. She'd kick my ass if I started tagging again."

I watched in amazement as Reid easily slipped into the role of authority figure, and much to my surprise the kids were actually responsive. I could tell the little punk talking to Reid with his pants around his knees probably gave his real teachers all kinds of grief but he clearly worshiped Reid.

"Yes, I've met your mother and I know very well what she would do to you if you were to tag Mr. Sinclair's craft store again." Reid said, crossing his arms in front of him and smirking at the kid.

"I got a bum rap without one, man. Know what I'm sayin', yo? You'd think he'd appreciate the artistic value." I had to look away so I wouldn't laugh. The kid was a character; of that I was sure.

"We talked about this before, Dougie fresh," Reid said with chuckle, I could practically hear the air quotes he mentally put around the boy's nickname. "There's a time and a place for your art, just make sure that you're not destroying other people's property when you do it, okay?"

"You got it, Mr. Reid. Now come on and see the tag," he said excitedly.

"I'll be right over. I want to introduce Briar to somebody."

Reid led me around the back of the room to where a girl was sitting by herself. Her long, dark hair had fallen to the side and obscured her face as she hunched over a sketchpad.

"Emma?" Reid asked in a gentle tone. Her head bounced up in surprise like she hadn't heard him walking in the room.

"Oh, h-hey Reid," she stuttered, casting her eyes back down to the sketch she'd been working on.

"Hey Emma, I just wanted to introduce you

to Briar. I was telling her about your work at the pizza parlor and she was interested in looking at some of your stuff. Would that be okay?"

"Oh sure," Emma said, nodding politely as she got up from her seat.

"I'll make my rounds and come back to check on you guys in a little bit," he added to Emma's back, she was already on her way over to the filing cabinet on the other side of the room. Unsure of what to do, I trailed behind her.

She took out a set of keys from her back pocket and opened the middle drawer pulling out a huge binder and slamming the drawer closed again. I followed her back to her deserted table and took the seat across from where she'd been working. Emma dropped the binder on the table, the smack it made caused the table to shake.

She flinched and her eyes widened as the entire room turned to stare, "Oops, sorry I didn't mean to," she winced and quickly took her seat again, keeping her head down.

I caught Reid's worried look in our direction and gave him a reassuring smile. "It's fine," I said quietly turning back to Emma and trying my best to sooth her anxiety. She seemed a little skittish. "So, Reid was telling me how awesome of an artist you are. I can't wait to see some of your work."

She gestured to the binder in front of me, "There are sketches and pictures of some of the bigger pieces I've done in there."

It was difficult at first, the conversation

stilted, but she eventually started to open up. By the time Reid came back to check on us we were halfway through her binder and she was giggling at all of my commentary.

"Look," I said, "I don't know much about art but this stuff is really good."

"Thanks," she said, giving me a pinched smile, as if she didn't quite believe me. I wasn't trying to be nice I was serious, the girl had talent. There were pencil sketches and pictures of huge canvas paintings she'd done. Everything from realistic portraits to abstract paintings full of color and movement.

Reid took a seat across the table from us, "So Emma, how'd the math test go yesterday?"

"Like shit," she said. I was surprised at the edge in her tone. The entire time we'd been talking she had been quiet and respectful but as soon as Reid brought up the subject of school she got that snarky sarcastic tone that only a teenager could pull off.

Reid didn't seem to notice or had just decided to ignore it as he continued to question her. "Did you study?" he asked gently.

She let out a frustrated sigh complete with an expertly executed eye roll, "There's no point in studying, I just don't get it. I'm never going to use algebra ever in my entire freaking life."

At that point I decided to interject because I knew exactly where she was coming from, "No, you're not Emma. I am here to tell you as a 25-year-old woman I have never once used algebra in my daily adult life."

"See what I mean?" Emma asked Reid imploringly.

"But," I continued, "you still have to pass algebra. It's just a fact of life. If you don't pass, you don't graduate."

"That's not fair, if we don't actually use it why do we have to learn it?"

"Because life's not fair and adults just want to torture teenagers," I responded. Reid gave me a funny look but I just shrugged my shoulders. It was true. There was no point in learning algebra or calculus unless you were going to be a fucking scientist or mathematician but everyone still had to do it.

"Look Emma, it's a means to an end. You've got a pass to graduate so you can get into college."

"Right, well I'm not going to college so I don't really have to worry about it."

"Emma," Reid interjected in what I'd guessed was his teacher voice.
Damn that was sexy.

I was quickly brought back to the conversation before my thoughts could wander too far as he continued. "We talked about this, you're more than capable of making it to college."

"Who's going to pay for it? Because it sure as hell isn't my mom."

"There are scholarships, and grants, and student loans. There are all kinds of options, if you really want to go to college you can make it happen," I said.

Emma was shaking her head before I even finished, "I wouldn't even know where to start, and who's going to give a grant or scholarship to a girl who can't even pass fucking algebra?"

"Language," Reid warned.

"Sorry," she mumbled and started picking at one of her black painted nails.

I wasn't about to let her off that easy though. From what Reid, had said about this girl, she needed someone to fight for her. To make her see her own potential. "One that's focused on the arts. Show them your work, show them how hard you tried in your other subjects. Even if you're a solid C student there are still options. Trust me, there are plenty of opportunities out there, you can find something that fits you."

"But I'm still going to have to do math and English and all that other shit in college. So even if I pass high school, I have to figure out a way to do it all in college," she argued. Damn this girl really did believe she was hopeless.

"What about art school? I mean, it's your passion, so why would you go to school for something else?" I asked perplexed at where her train of thought was going.

"Look lady," she said exasperated.

Lady? Since when did I become a lady? Last time I checked I was barely an adult.

"I don't know how it is where you come

from, but I don't have the luxury of doing what I love and letting mommy and daddy pay my way," Emma lashed out, and I could tell Reid was getting uneasy with her rising voice, but I was up for the challenge.

"Okay, so say you don't pass high school, you don't go to college, and you don't do anything else with your art, what's your plan? What are you going do to make a living?" I asked.

"I don't know. I guess I'll pick up some more shifts at the diner or something."

"Is that really how you want to spend the rest your life?"

"No one *wants* to be a waitress," she replied angrily, her face starting to redden but she continued, "I appreciate what you're doing but not everyone's destined for greatness. Someone's got to pour the coffee."

"What are you doing after school tomorrow?" I asked suddenly, as a brilliant plan started to formulate in the back of my head. This girl reminded me so much of Alex when we were kids. The only chance I had of getting through to her was by showing her what her future could be like.

She furrowed her eyebrows, "My shift at the diner starts at six, why?"

"Okay, what time do you get off school?" I asked. Reid, who had remained mostly silent during our heated discussion, gave me a questioning look from across the table and I just smiled. I could tell they were both wondering where the fuck I was going with this.

"Three o'clock," she said suspiciously.

"Perfect." I ripped off a square of scratch paper and wrote down an address. "Meet me here at 3:30 tomorrow."

She rolled her eyes again. If there was an Olympic event for eye rolling she would be a serious contender. "Why?"

"Because I have someone I want you to meet." I said simply, needing to punish the little shit a bit for arguing with me.

She just shrugged her shoulders and took the address, "Fine."

I could see Reid out of the corner of my eye staring at me, but I ignored him. "I'll see you there tomorrow. Just so you know, if you don't show up, I'll hunt you down. Understood?"

"Jesus, yeah lady I'll be there," her monotone voice droned out, but the curve at the corner of her lips gave away the smile she was suppressing.

Ha! She's breaking. This is going to be easier than I'd thought.

We stayed for another hour, spending time with each of the kids. I was riding a sort of high as we headed out. They were all so excited to show someone new what they'd been working on and I couldn't help but get into it. Not all the kids had Emma's talent, but they were all enthusiastic, and they adored Reid. I couldn't blame them; he was pretty great.

"I can see why you volunteer," I said to Reid as we walked down the hallway towards the main entrance. "I kind of feel like I might be able to make a difference for Emma. If I can just show her the opportunities out there for her, maybe she'll see that she's got actual potential to do something other than sling French fries for a living."

"I hope so, nothing I've done has worked. I don't want her to get lost in the shuffle, she's a good ki—" Reid said but before he could finish his thought a blonde woman came hustling around the corner and nearly took us out.

"Oh shoot, sorry!" she said in a rush, out of breath. She stood up straight and smoothed out her shirt before looking up at us again, "Oh my gosh, Reid!"

"Nova, hey! It's been a long time," Reid said easily. They knew each other? Apparently, since he leaned in and gave her a quick hug. When they separated, I had to tamp down the urge to pee all over him and yell 'MINE!'

"Nova, I'd like you to meet my—" Reid said, attempting to introduce me. I panicked and interrupted him before he got a chance to finish.

"Briar, nice to meet you," I said shaking her hand. We hadn't had the exclusivity conversation and I'd be damned if I was going to have that conversation in front of a goddamn super model.

With her heels on she was a good five inches taller than me. My eyes traveled down the length of her, trying to be inconspicuous as I sized her up. She was dressed in a cream blouse, black slacks, and a perfectly posh pearl necklace and earrings. The girl was the complete opposite of me; tall, perfectly styled blonde hair, clear blue eyes, and runway model skinny. She was drop-dead fucking gorgeous.

I kind of felt like it was only fair to the rest of the world if a person had a perfect body that they needed to have a horse face or something to even the playing field. I mean, it just wasn't fair to everybody else. If someone had everything going for them, then the least God could do was throw the rest of us a bone and give them a tail something.

I was no slouch in the looks department but I was distinctly thicker than the chick standing before me. We're talking size 0. No really, bitch needed to eat a fucking cheeseburger. She looked like she'd lived off of kale and beet juice for the past 12 years.

"So nice to meet you," she said, and goddamn it the bitch's voice was musical. I'd heard of a voice being described in books as musical before, but I'd never actually heard what it sounded like until that moment. It was like I was in the goddamn sound of music, I half expected everyone around me to break out in song and dance.

"Nova," Reid interrupted my thoughts. "I haven't seen you in forever, what are you doing here?"

"I just moved here a few months ago. I liked the work we did together at the youth center in Bend so much I figured I'd do some volunteer work here too."

Bend. So, she knew Reid from before. I'm so fucking confused right now, how the hell does he know this fucking supermodel?

"I didn't know you moved here, it's so great to see you," Reid said. "Is Brad with you?"

"Umm, yeah. Brad's still in Bend. We called it quits actually," she said looking a little embarrassed.

"Oh no, I'm so sorry to hear that," Reid said with genuine concern. I started to feel a little bad for judging this woman, but as soon as Reid reached out and placed a comforting hand on her shoulder all the pity I was beginning to feel flew right out the window.

Funny how that happens.

"It's for the best. Anyway, I decided to move to the big city for a change of pace," she said.

"Good for you," Reid said.

"We'll have to get together for drinks sometime?" she asked looking between both of us hopefully. "I don't know anyone here and it'd be nice to meet some new people and catch up of course."

"Absolutely. In fact, we're having a Halloween party at Bearded Jack's this Saturday at eight, you should come."

She knew where he worked? I thought they hadn't seen each other in years? This was getting more and more confusing by the minute.

"That sounds great!" she said excitedly and looked down at her watch, which in case you were wondering was rose gold and probably worth more than my car. "Shoot, I've got to run. It was very nice meeting you Briar. Reid, so happy I ran into you. See you this weekend," she called over her shoulder as she rushed off in the direction we'd just come from.

I wanted to hate her, I really did. It wasn't fair for someone to be that beautiful and also be that fucking sweet. It made me want to gag on my own vomit.

"See you then!" I called after her, a little too enthusiastically. I didn't want her to think that I was a bitch. I mean, I was a bitch. but I didn't want her to know that. At least not until I figured out what the hell was going on with her and Reid.

I kept my mouth shut as we were leaving the building. I didn't want to come out and ask him how he knew her. In a perfect world, he'd bring it up casually and explain the situation so I wouldn't have to sound like a jealous girlfriend. Not that I was his girlfriend, at least not technically. For the second time in less than an hour, the thought occurred to me that we hadn't had any sort of conversation about where we stood with each other.

My mind instantly started to spiral down the rabbit hole, what if he was seeing other people? I hadn't so much as texted another guy since our first date.

Shit! Now on top of the 'who the fuck was that' talk we also had to have the 'what are we' talk. I needed a fucking drink.

"I know you want to ask so just ask," Reid broke through my panicked thoughts as soon as we got into the car.

"I don't know what you're talking about," I said, trying to sound nonchalant.

"I call bullshit," he said, his tone was even but he gave me a smile so that I knew he was joking.

"Okay fine, who is she?" I asked, a little disgruntled that he was forcing me to ask instead of just telling me what we both knew I wanted to know.

He laughed under his breath, and shook his head, "We grew up together, our parents are friends, I've known her since we were in diapers."

"Have you slept with her?" I asked.

Reid hung his head and chuckled, "Yeah, we dated a very long time ago, throughout high school, it was forever ago."

"High school, huh?" I asked, "So you guys haven't hooked up since then?" I added a slight teasing tone to my words in an effort to take the edge of jealousy out of them.

"What? God, no. We ended things on a friendly note before college. There were no hard feelings or anything like that. Hell, up until apparently just a few months ago, she was engaged to this guy Brad that we went to high school with and they'd been together since college. Trust me, Nova and I were kids when we dated, it wasn't serious."

"Okay, I believe you. I just had to ask."

"I would expect nothing less from you," he said with a wink and lifted the hand he'd intertwined with mine during our conversation and brought it to his lips.

God, I loved it when he did that.

Nineteen

Boyfriend Trifecta

"So what do you want to do?" Reid asked as we pulled out of the parking lot.

"I don't know. Alex is at the shop for the rest of the day and Evie's with her dad at the gym so no one's home. Do want to go back to my place and watch a movie or something?"

"Did you just Netflix and chill me?" he asked incredulously.

I thought about it for a minute before I responded, "Why yes, yes I did."

"Well alright then, at least you're being honest," Reid said and took the turn towards my house.

***

We sat at opposite ends of the couch as I

surfed Netflix. It was awkward to say the least, which was so out of character for Reid and I. We'd developed this easy rhythm, which was nowhere to be found at the moment. Even though there was only three feet separating us it felt like a lot more. I didn't know how to act. We were in this limbo stage. We'd spent a lot of time together in the past few weeks and even more time talking on the phone, but we'd never been completely alone like this. The tension in the room caused me to be hyper-aware of every twitch, inhale, and shift coming from his side.

Reid was the first to break the awkward silence, "You know, I'm kind of pissed at you."

"What? Why?" I asked.

"You didn't let me introduce you as my girlfriend at the volunteer center."

You know that moment in movies where the record stops and everything comes to a screeching halt? Yeah, it was nothing like that.

"What?" I squeaked, turning my whole body towards him. "What are you talking about?" My voice coming out high-pitched and wobbly. I didn't know why I was reacting this way. I had known that was probably where he was going today but I figured we'd wait to have the conversation until after we'd had a few drinks and the unusual stiffness we were feeling had faded away.

"When I tried, you cut me off and didn't let me finish."

"I didn't know I was your girlfriend?" It came out as more of a question than the statement it was meant to be.

"You are. Do you have a problem with that?" he asked, and it took me a minute to register his words.

Wasn't this supposed to be a conversation?

I just stared, unblinking at him and he stared right back. I had never seen this side of Reid before. Gone was my goofy, fun loving Reid. Replaced by the serious, albeit sexy, version sitting in front of me. He hadn't asked me, he'd told me what I was to him, only asking if I objected.

I decided to ignore the part of me that found this new, commanding side of him all sorts of panty dropping sexy and instead focused on the part that was freaking the fuck out.

It wasn't that I'd never been someone's girlfriend before. I'd been graced with the title plenty of times, but with Reid I knew it meant more than it had with my previous boyfriends. I desperately needed to figure out something witty to say to lighten the mood because I was not prepared for the deep water the conversation was headed towards.

"Aren't boyfriends supposed to put out?" I asked, only halfway teasing because honestly, this guy had to give it up at some point.

Reid's serious expression broke with a laugh, "Yeah, I guess you're right."

I jumped up from the couch and stood in

front of him pumping my fist in the air and cheering, "Hallelujah, praise Jesus! He's finally going to give it up!" I shouted, "Now, can he live up to the anticipation?"

Reid unfolded himself from the couch and stood to his full height, towering over me with a mischievous glint in his eye as I continued to tease him. I'd never given much thought to how much taller he was than me, except for the fact that he could reach things I couldn't. He'd proved himself and his go-go gadget arms useful time and again. As he stared down at me, an overwhelming sense of desire pulsed through my body, but I wasn't going to let that stop me from heckling him.

"Can he do it folks? Can his performance meet expectations?" I asked, using my best sports announcer voice. My jeering was brought to a sudden stop with the loud smack on my behind. My head whipped up, my mouth hanging open. Reid's heated gaze clashed with my shocked one. For once in my life I was speechless.

"Why don't you get your ass in your room and I'll show you," he said in a deep voice that I had never heard before, it was barely above a growl and it made my thoughts go haywire.

Holy sweet mother of God, it's always the ones you least expect.

He just quirked an eyebrow at me expectantly while I stared at him wide-eyed. Was he fucking serious? I started to walk towards my bedroom slowly, I still wasn't completely convinced he wasn't joking. But a look over my shoulder made it clear he was completely serious by the way he was stalking after me. Jesus Christ, what happened to my sweet funny Reid? Could it be true? Had I found the boyfriend trifecta? Funny, charming, and hot as hell in bed? Oh, God, I hoped so.

As we crossed the threshold of my bedroom I froze, standing still in the middle of the room with my back to Reid who I heard step into the room a second after I did. For the first time since I lost my virginity when I was fifteen to Jesse Bowman, I had no idea what the fuck I was supposed to do. Do I initiate? What happens next? Do I take charge or let him?

My questions dissolved when I felt Reid come up behind me, his warm chest pressing into my back. Wrapping his arms around my waist, his hands found their way under my shirt to lay flat on my belly. Nuzzling my neck with his nose, he began pressing soft kisses from my shoulder up my neck. I tilted my head, giving him better access as he trailed closer to my ear. He nipped at my ear before he whispered, "What do you want?"

The instant the words left his lips my mind went blank. I was never at a loss for words in the bedroom, I always had a quick-witted retort or a sexy something to say. I considered myself a modern woman and wasn't afraid to tell my partner what I wanted and how I wanted it. At the moment, though, I couldn't think of a single thing to say. What did I want? I felt like anything I said to

Reid at this point would carry a much heavier meaning than what was intended and I wasn't sure I was ready for that.

Reid must have noticed my discomfort, because he turned me around and put his hands on either side of my face, searching my eyes before he spoke, "Briar, sweetheart. We don't have to do anything if you're not ready."

His words instantly dislodge all reservations, "No!" it came out louder than I'd intended and I winced. "I want to, I just I don't know how we do this," I said motioning back and forth between us. I was clueless. Our relationship thus far had been about getting to know one another and having fun. We'd built a friendship but the physical aspect of our relationship was solely comprised of a few stolen kisses and some lingering hugs. Fuck, what if we'd inadvertently friend zoned each other?

Reid seemed to understand my rambling because his eyes softened. "Relax, stop over thinking everything," he said, pressing a close-mouthed kiss to my lips.

I tried to do what he said and relax but I couldn't. I cared about what he thought of me. I'd had sex with my fair share of men but I never really cared what they thought of me and never experienced this sort of hesitation when it came to the actual sex part. I realized what was happening with Reid was more, taking this step meant more.

It wasn't just sex. We were starting a

relationship. A relationship that looked nothing like any I'd ever had because all my previous relationships had been based on sex, and subsequently failed because we weren't compatible outside the bedroom. It was the complete opposite with Reid. We'd formed a foundation, and now the stakes were higher, because as awesome as our time had been leading up to this, what happened next could make or break it.

Is this what men experience when they talk about performance anxiety? Shit, this was karma rearing her bitchy head because of all the shit I'd said to Reid before. I was so screwed.

"Stop," Reid said, smiling down at me. He brushed my hair off of one shoulder, cupping my jaw with his hand and threading the other through my hair at the nape of my neck.

He kissed the corners of my mouth, his thumb gently caressing my jaw and my nerves started to dissolve. His sweet kisses turned into nips and I gasped in surprise when he gave the hand holding my hair a slight tug. Taking the opportunity my parted lips granted, he deepened the kiss, his tongue darting past my lips. I let out an involuntarily moan when his tongue touched mine and I arched against him pressing my chest to his. I could feel my nipples tighten under the friction.

We kissed for a long while, all the anxiety draining from my body as he alternated between soft sweeps of his tongue and sharp bites to my lower lip. The hand that was cradling my jaw made its way down to my waist and pulled me closer. He pressed his hips forward to meet mine and a small whimper escaped my throat.

Releasing my hair, his other hand traveled down to my backside, giving my ass a light squeeze. I reacted immediately, sliding my hands that had been resting on his strong chest up and around his neck. My fingers slipping over the short hair at the back of his head and climbing higher to grab a fistful of hair where it was longer on top. He growled when I tugged, and bent down quickly wrapping a hand around each of my thighs right below my ass and picking me up. I let out a yelp of surprise and quickly wrapped my legs around his middle, locking my ankles together.

Reid walked us over to the bed and laid me gently down, but he didn't untangle himself from me. Instead he loomed over me on his elbows, his arms caging me in. My skin felt hot, my heartbeat was racing and I couldn't get close enough as I continued to kiss and paw at him. I wanted to get closer. Resting his weight on one arm he lowered a hand between us, edging the hem of my shirt up to just below my breast, his thumb sweeping across my ribs back and forth, back and forth.

The feel of his skin on mine was intoxicating, I wanted more. Reaching down I scrunched up his shirt on his back and let my hands wander, but it wasn't enough. I pulled on the fabric that had quickly become my worst enemy. He replied to my silent indication and I melted into the bed as I watched him sit up and reach between his shoulders pulling his shirt off over his head. There was nothing sexier than watching a guy take off his shirt like that, something about the sheer manliness of it made all my lady parts pay attention.

I'd never seen him without a shirt on, I took my time letting my eyes wander. He was all lean muscle, not quite a six-pack but he had the deep V lines that pointed straight to what I hoped would be my happy place. Reaching up, I ran a finger across one pierced nipple and then repeated the action on the other. I had known he had these, I'd felt them through a shirt a couple of times, they were sexy as hell.

I continued to explore his chest running my fingers over the huge eagle tattoo that was centered on his chest. It was done in the traditional old-school style with heavy lines and bold colors. My hands traced the wings all the way up and over his shoulders and back again. Letting my fingernails drag across his ribs I watched in fascination as his stomach contracted at my touch. My fingertips dipped into the lines of defined muscle and followed them all the way down, hooking them into the waistband of his jeans.

Reid braced himself above me with his hands on either side of my head as I thumbed open the button on his jeans and slowly pulled the zipper down, my hands shaking. He must have noticed my nervousness because his big hand encircled one of my wrists, stilling my journey to the promised land. Dammit.

"Not yet," he whispered, sitting back on his knees and pulling me up with him. He slowly lifted my shirt up and over my head.

Leaning forward, he kissed me softly and pulled back, gliding a finger down the delicate lace on my bra strap and across one cup causing goose bumps to irrupt all over my body. Lust flashed in his eyes as the other hand reached behind my back and deftly unhooked the clasp. His hands smoothed down my arms as he brought both straps down and removed my bra, flinging it behind him. His nostrils flared and I noticed his jaw clench when he saw my breasts bared to him for the first time. My heart was thundering in my chest and my brain was cloudy, the nerves that had faded before came rushing back tenfold as he sat there and stared at my body.

"You're so beautiful," he whispered reverently. In that moment, with him staring at me with hope and wonder in his eyes, I realized I'd never felt more naked in my entire life. Not just physically, but emotionally. I was well on my way to giving this man the power to break me, and no matter how much I tried to prevent it he found a way to sneak past every barrier.

A chill of anticipation ran up my spine as I reached forward and placed my hands on his chest skating them up and around to pull him down for a searing kiss. It was as if my kiss was the shotgun start of the race. Hands and lips were everywhere. Reid reach down and pulled off my leggings and underwear in one swift motion, taking my socks with. In just a moment I was completely naked laying before him, but I didn't give him time to take his fill.   I reach forward pushing down his underwear and jeans, eager to see what he'd been holding out on me.

The first thing I saw when he was released from his pants was a flash of metal. My eyes flew up to his and I quirked an eyebrow. "What's this?" I asked, my voice husky with lust.

"It's an apadravya," he said, "trust me, you'll like it." I let my eyes wander back down and inspect the piece of jewelry, a silver barbell with the two balls nestled on the top and underside of the head. I licked my lips and moved to lean down, wanting to get a taste of the bead of pre-come glistening at his tip but he put a hand on my shoulder to stop me.

"As much as I want your mouth on me that's not going to happen right now," I looked up at him with a little pout on my face, I didn't normally pout but what the fuck was wrong with this guy? Was delayed gratification all that great? "Don't give me that look, trust me you'll get your opportunity, but if you put that dirty little mouth around my cock now it'll be over before we even get started. Besides, I want to taste you."

Well, I couldn't argue with that. I gave him

a mischievous grin and leaned back on the bed. He leaned back over me kissing a trail from my neck down my chest, paying extra attention to each peek and slowly let his lips travel down around my belly button and even further. He slid off the bed until he was kneeling on the floor in front of me. Wrapping a hand around each leg he pulled me sharply towards him causing my whole body to slide across the bed to his waiting mouth. He hitched one of my legs over his shoulder and wasted no time sweeping his tongue over my most sensitive parts.

I bowed off the bed the instant his tongue touched my clit. My pulse was quick and my gasps were short. "Jesus, fuck!" I muttered. He was good, really fucking good.

I felt myself building and building, getting closer and closer to the edge with the deft movements of his tongue and when he added two fingers, my orgasm tore through my veins like wildfire. My muscles seized as I shattered apart with a scream ripping through my throat.

When I slumped back onto the bed my lungs burned and my heart was beating wildly in my chest. It was the most intense orgasm I'd ever had, and it left me completely wrung out. My over sensitized skin buzzed everywhere Reid touched me as he slid his hands back up my body and kissed his way to my lips. It took me a minute to come back down to reality. When I peeled my eyes, open Reid was hovering above me placing soft kisses on my face. I stared at him in amazement. I had never had a man bring me to orgasm that quickly. It felt like I was ready to explode at the first stroke of his tongue.

"Wow," I said. It was the only thing I *could* say. He was a hell of a lot better than I had even hoped for. Reid gave me a slightly cocky smirk and continued to kiss me. I felt his tongue brush across my lips and I opened my mouth to let him in. As soon as I tasted myself on his tongue my body lit up again. There was something so sexy about tasting my own desire on him. I wrapped my legs around his waist and pulled him further onto me. He tried to hold himself up, as not to put all of his weight on me, but I wasn't having it. I pulled hard until he was laying flush against me. I felt the barbell that adorned his cock brush up against my sensitive clit and let out a small gasp.

Reid tilted back his hips and aligned himself before he started to press forward but then froze. "Shit," he mumbled, "Condom."

I just shook my head, he felt too good to stop now, "I'm clean and I'm on the pill. We're good."

He pulled back and looked me in the eye, as if assessing whether I was sure. "I am too. Clean that is, not on the pill," he stuttered. "Are you sure?" he asked, hesitation in his voice.

"Yeah," I whispered and lifted my head to kiss him again. I didn't want anything between us, and I trusted him. In that moment giving him my trust meant more to me than I wanted to think about.

He kissed me deeply and pushed inside. It was a tight fit, especially with the balls, but I was slick from when he'd worked me over before. I inhaled sharply when he bottomed out, followed by a loud moan.

"Fuck!" he grated out. "You're so fucking tight," he said, through heavy breaths, stilling inside me, "Goddamn, so wet."

I clenched my internal muscles to encourage him to move, I needed him to move.

"Briar, Jesus. Don't do that," he gasped, he was struggling to control himself, but I wasn't about to let him off, I needed him to move or I was going to lose it.

"What?" I asked, kissing up the column of his neck, "This?" I questioned innocently, and did it again. He growled and started to move, finally. Increasing his pace faster and faster until he was pounding into me hard and my eyes were practically rolling into the back of my head. Each thrust punctuated by a moan from me or a grunt from him. He hitched one of my legs up higher, changing the angle and pressing even deeper than before. The new angle made the little balls rub and drag across just the right spots, making me see stars. I felt the familiar pull in my lower belly and knew I was close again.

He must've felt the change in me as my climax started to build because he whispered in my ear, his breath ragged with exertion, "Come for me." My body flushed at his words and my blood became hot in my veins. He punctuated every thrust with a grind of his body against mine causing him to rub deliciously against my clit each time. He bit down hard on my neck and I felt my orgasm roll through me until I exploded into a million pieces. As soon as I started to fall apart Reid doubled his efforts, thrusting faster and harder than he had before, chasing his own release.

Reid lay on top of me, careful not to crush me with his full weight, his face buried in my hair as he caught his breath. My hands roamed over his sweat-slicked back, drawing lazy circles as I floated in my post-orgasm bliss. After a while, when our bodies had cooled and our breaths had returned to normal he pulled out of me and rolled onto his back beside me. I instantly missed the contact but I didn't have time to process that thought because just then, Reid pulled me to him, situating me so I was sprawled out on top of him.

Then, the worst thing that could ever happen after the first time you had sex with someone happened.

I queefed. Loudly.

I was momentarily frozen; I couldn't believe what I'd just heard. Sure, it was a normal bodily function and it happened sometimes after sex but no matter how much I knew logically it was normal and I hadn't done anything wrong, I was still mortified.

"Br—" Reid started to say something, but I cut him off.

"You hungry?" I asked hurriedly, reaching down to grab my leggings off the floor. It's not that I wanted to hurry up and get rid of him, I didn't. I just didn't want to have the awkward conversation about sex noises. We didn't need it. I was going to pretend it never happened and pray he'd get sudden onset amnesia. No sense in making things weird.

"I could eat, what did you have in mind?" he responded easily, seeming to catch on to my need for a diversion and reached down to grab his own jeans.

"Don't know yet. Depends if the savages have raided the fridge this week or not."

"Savages?"

"Kellen and Knox," I grumbled. He'd heard me complain about the pair of them enough to understand.

I slipped on a hoodie and headed out to the kitchen with Reid on my heels. As soon as we made it to the end of the hall there was an eruption of cheering and clapping. I froze in horror as Alex, Evie, and Knox stood in the living room hooting and fist pumping while my brother sat on the couch scowling. Fuck.

Twenty

Tattoos and Dirty Bitches

I looked down at my phone for the fourth time in five minutes. She was late. What was it with artists being late? Was that a thing? Like their minds were too full of creative shit and they just couldn't be bothered to remember bland things like punctuality. Alex was the same way. I swear to God that woman would be late to her own funeral, the only thing she was ever on time for was work.

Says the woman that got fired for being late to work.

To be fair, I fucking hated that job. I was about to check my phone again when I spotted Emma running full speed up the sidewalk.

"Hey," she wheezed, bending at the waist and resting her hands on her knees as she tried to catch her breath.

"Hey yourself, did you run all the way

here?" I asked genuinely concerned. She was huffing and puffing like the goddamned big bad wolf on crack.

"Sorry, I missed my bus and had to catch another one that dropped me off a few blocks farther down. I ran the rest of the way here."

"No worries. You ready to go in?" I asked gesturing to the door behind me. She straightened and looked up at the building, her brow furrowing in confusion.

"You had me meet you at a tattoo studio? I'm underage..." she trailed off.

I laughed, "No, it's not like that. I have someone I want you to meet. Did you bring your book?"

She hoisted her backpack further up on her shoulders, "Yup, just like you asked."

"Alright, let's go," I said and pushed into the studio.

The bell above the door chimed as we walked in, the sound of buzzing needles hits my ears instantly. Two leather couches and a small coffee table made up the small waiting area, and the walls were plastered in sketches by the artists that worked at the studio. I glanced at Emma as she took in the room. Her expression was hesitant at first, as if she didn't know what to do with herself. But as soon as she caught sight of the framed sketches on the walls her expression changed to wonder. I laughed when she gravitated toward the wall of Alex's sketches to get a better look.

"Hey, Briar," a voice called out behind me. I turned to see Wes standing behind the reception desk and if the sharp intake of breath from my right was any indication, Emma saw him too. Wes was the resident apprentice at the shop. He'd been around for about a year and was hotter than sin. For a child, anyway, at nineteen he was way too young for me. I wasn't ready to be a cougar yet, but from the reaction Emma was having to just the sight of him, she was all about the older men.

"I didn't see you on the schedule but Alex has some time if you want to work on your side piece," he announced as he flipped through the schedule book, completely oblivious to the teenage girl who was drooling all over herself in front of him.

"It's all good, I'm just bringing Emma here to meet with Alex."

Wes looked up from the schedule book and flashed a full toothed smile at her. "Hey, I'm Wes, nice to meet you," he walked around the desk and extended his hand for her to shake. She stared at him unblinking for about two seconds before I nudged her with my elbow, which caused her to break out of her lust induced trance.

"Oh, uh, yeah. Hi, I'm Em-Emma," she stuttered, taking his hand for a quick shake. I kind of felt bad for not warning her ahead of time, but I'd forgotten what it was like to be a teenager in the presence of the uber hot bad boy.

"So, are you interested in getting some

work done?" he asked taking her in and giving her a grin. Oh, dear God, he was flirting with her, go Emma! Her blush had risen from her cheeks to the roots of her dark hair and she was fiddling with the strap of her bag.

"Uh, actually I'm not old enough yet," she said shyly and I watched as all the cocky interest in Wes' face faded into shock and he took a deliberate step away from her.

"Right, well Alex is just finishing up with a client. She should be out in a minute," he said making his way back behind the desk.

"Emma is an artist actually," I said. "That's why we're here. I want Alex to talk to her about her options for continuing with her art after she graduates in a few months." Good job, Briar. That wasn't obvious at all.

"Really?" Wes asked, but there was no heat in his eyes when he looked at Emma again, just professional curiosity.

Dammit, no dice.

"It's just something I like," she shrugged. "I'm not good enough to make money or anything—"

"Wes, have you ever been to Zombie Eats?"

"The pizza place on Hawthorne?" he asked, giving me a weird look, probably wondering where I was going with the sudden subject change.

"Yeah, you know that mural they have? She did it," I said nodding in Emma's direction.

"No shit?" he asked surprised.

"Yeah, it's no big deal," she said, shuffling her feet and if it was possible her blush got even deeper.

Just then, Alex emerged from the back room with a giant shirtless man on her heels. I tried not to laugh at the way Emma's eyes bulged out of her head when she saw the tatted-up hulk. He walked around to the front of the reception desk to settle his bill and we got a clear view of the enormous back piece Alex had been working on through the saran wrap she'd covered it with to protect the freshly inked skin.

Two dragons took up either side of his back and met in the middle as if they were facing off. One side was surrounded in water while the other was engulfed in flames. It was totally bad ass. He put his shirt back on as Alex went over the care instructions and scheduled a follow up appointment.

"Bye Gabe, I'll see you in a few weeks," Alex called out as the brute of a man left. She spotted us and made her way over. "Hey, you must be Emma, I'm Alex," she said taking Emma's hand and giving her a warm smile.

"Nice to meet you," Emma said, ducking her head.

We need to work on this girl's social skills.

"Why don't you guys come on back and we can chat," Alex said, leading us down a hallway towards the back of the shop.

"I can't believe you know one of the artists,"

Emma whispered.

"Know her? I live with her," I laughed.

"You are way cooler than I thought you were," Emma responded in awe.

What the fuck was that supposed to mean? Since when did I go from judging others for their cool status to being judged? This adulting thing blows.

"Look, I know you're not into the college thing right now. I get it, but hear what she has to say. Listen to her story and then decide what you want to do. Okay?"

"Sure," she nodded as we entered Alex's small room. Emma gravitated towards the art on the walls, her eyes bouncing from one colorful piece to the next.

"Have a seat," Alex said, gesturing to the tattoo chair she'd just finished wiping down. "Briar tells me you're an artist, is that right?"

"Yeah, I guess," Emma responded timidly.

I simultaneously wanted to beat my head against the wall, shake Emma, and cry for her. She had zero self-confidence and it broke my cold, black heart.

"Bullshit," I called out, "she's amazing."

"Briar," Alex said exasperated, "some artists are humble, I know that's hard for you to believe..."

"What the fuck ever, you are the least humble person I know so cut the crap, and you," I said turning to Emma, "need to start believing that you have talent." Reaching down to where Emma had set her bag, I opened it and pulled out her binder, placing it next to her on the chair.

"Holy crap," Alex said pulling the binder closer and flipping through it. "How long have you been doing art?"

Emma looked down at her hands before she spoke, "Well, I mean I've been sketching forever, but I guess a couple years ago when the program started at the Youth Center. Reid introduced me to different mediums and I really got into it after that."

I kind of zoned out when they started comparing thoughts on different styles and shading techniques while Alex combed through her portfolio. I came back around when they finally started saying shit I could understand.

"This is some impressive work, how old are you?" Alex asked.

"Seventeen, I'll be eighteen in June."

"Alex," I piped up, "why don't you tell her a little bit about your career and school?"

Alex sighed, giving me a 'shut the fuck up' look, and turned to Emma, "Your grades are shit, right?" she asked. I had to give it to her, she held nothing back, my girl was as straight forward as they came.

"Yeah, pretty much. Which is why I keep telling Briar not to waste her breath, I'm not going to college."

Wait a minute, since when did I become the

bad guy?

"Math or science?" Alex asked, not giving in to the diversion.

"Both," Emma mumbled sheepishly.

"Yeah, I had the same problem. I was fine with English and History, but equations and formulas," she clucked her tongue, "not something that my brain could process. I always had an interest in art and I was good at it so I applied for art school and got in. I knew from the time I was eighteen and got my first piece that I wanted to be a tattoo artist. Since I already knew what I wanted to do, I focused on sketching and shading, anything that would make me better at this kind of art. I met Gavin at a showcase the school put on and he let me come apprentice for him."

"Gavin?" Emma asked.

"He owns the shop. He's enjoying his partial retirement. I run things when he's not around."

"That's so cool. I've never thought about being a tattoo artist."

"It's fucking amazing. I make it sound easy but trust me, it was hard. A lot of long hours and not a lot of glory, but being able to tattoo fresh skin for the very first time, there's nothing like it. When a client trusts you to put something that you created permanently on their body it's a total rush." Alex prattled on about becoming an apprentice and what it took to become a tattoo artist. She made plans with Emma to take her around the Art Institute and have her meet some people while I thumbed through Emma's drawings.

Last night I'd been thinking about a way that I could show Emma that I believed in her since it was clear to me that nobody else ever had. Of course, Reid did, but I don't think that counted for Emma in the same way because he was her teacher. She wanted approval and she needed it from somebody else. Somebody outside of her bubble.

"Can you guys chat about this while I get some work done?" I asked, interrupting their conversation.

"Sure, you want to make some progress on your side? I have about two hours before my next client."

Finding the picture that I was looking for, I swiveled it around and showed them. "I want that," I said.

"What?" Emma squeaked, "You want my drawing?"

I just shrugged like it was no big deal, "I like it."

"Are you sure?" she asked, "it's just something I was messing around with."

"Yes, I'm sure. Now go sit over there so you can watch how it all works," I said motioning for her to hop off the chair. Alex gave me a knowing smile as she started to set up and I smirked back at her.

"It'll just take me a few minutes to draw it up, then we can start. Do you want color or black and gray?" Alex asked as she traced the drawing onto a piece of transfer paper.

"What do you think Emma, black and gray or color?"

Emma hesitated for a second. She had a hopeful look on her face, as if she wanted to be excited but didn't want to show it and look uncool.

Fucking teenagers.

"Well, the picture is done in charcoal so I guess I'd go with black and gray."

"Black and gray it is," I said with a nod and Emma's face lit up.

"Where do you want it?" Alex asked when she'd finished tracing.

"I'm thinking my left hip, what do you think?"

"That works, you don't really have anything on that side. You could probably expand on it or work it into another piece down the road if you want to."

"Perfect, let's do this. Don't mind my pale ass," I said shimmying down my pants.

"First things first," Alex explained, "You have to wash the skin and make sure it's clean otherwise the transfer won't stick and you run the risk of infection. Especially when you're working on a dirty bitch like this."

"Go fuck yourself," I huffed.

Alex continued to explain the process to Emma step-by-step as she transferred the template and started putting needle to flesh. She told her about the different types of needles and everything else she could think of as she worked on me. Emma had to leave for her shift at the diner before Alex was finished with the tattoo but I promised her I'd stop by the Youth Center the next day and show her the work. After a quick goodbye and a slightly awkward hug as I was still laying on the table, Emma left.

"That was a pretty cool thing you did for her," Alex murmured as she wiped away some excess ink from my skin.

"What? I just liked the drawing," I responded casually.

"You know what I mean, dickhead. This means more to her than you can possibly imagine. Trust me, I know, I've been in her shoes."

"Whatever, let's not get all mushy now. She just needed someone to show her that her art is something more than just pencil and paper. She's got to realize there's more in her future than just waiting tables and serving coffee. If this is what does it then that's great. If not, then I have an awesome new tattoo."

***

I walked into Bearded Jack's and spotted Reid immediately at the bar. Sneaking up behind him, I covered his eyes. "Guess who."

"Wait, don't tell me, Jessica? No, no, no, Miranda?"

"Hardy har, har, very funny," I said, taking the stool next to him.

"Oh come on, I was just teasing. I knew it was you, Jessica's hands are a lot softer than yours."

"You Sir, are a twat." I knew it wasn't exactly normal to call your boyfriend a twat but Reid barely noticed my colorful vocabulary anymore. Although, he still blushed when I talked dirty to him in public, something I took immense joy in doing as often as I could.

"Seriously though, how did it go?"

"It went really well actually, I even got some new ink."

"Where? I want to see," Reid asked, his eyes searching my exposed skin for evidence.

"Maybe later, *if* you play your cards right," I said waggling my eyebrows.

"I'll be on my best behavior, scouts honor. So, do you think it changed her mind about college?"

"I don't know yet. I think she's definitely interested in tattooing now, but she's still hesitant about school. I think she's scared. Alex is going to take her to the school, show her around and introduce her to some people she knows there. Then it's her decision."

"You're good at this," he said, smiling at me.

"Good at what? Being pushy?"

"No, well yes, sort of," noticing my not so happy expression he back peddled. "I knew that if

207

you met Emma and looked at her drawings you would see her potential. You can be quite convincing when you want to be."

"Is that so?"

Reid laughed, "Yeah, I'd like to think that I'm becoming an expert on everything Briar Rose Jameson."

"You are so cheesy," I giggled. An actual, honest to God, giggle.

What the fuck is wrong with me? I do not giggle while sober, ever.

"You like it," Reid said, bending down to brush a kiss across my lips.

God help me, I kind of do.

Twenty-One

Insomnia and Emotional Immaturity

My head was buzzing and I couldn't shut it off. So instead of sleeping I was staring at the ceiling. Reid snoring lightly beside me like he didn't have a care in the world while I was tormented by what he was doing to me.

Bastard.

I liked the way he made me feel. I liked it a lot. The way his smile drew out my own. Even in protest, my lips responded to him, pulling up on their own accord into a shy smile. When he gave me that grin, the one that made the skin around his eyes crinkle and showed all his teeth. That smile brought out a stupid grin of my own. The kind that made my cheeks hurt.

I both loved and hated the effect he had on me. The way my chest would get tight and my stomach summersaulted. The way that when we were staring at each other and smiling like idiots it was as if nothing in the entire universe mattered more than the golden flecks in his green eyes and the fullness in my heart.

But as I stared into the darkness in the middle of the night, the fear began to set in. Like a deck of cards being shuffled, the questions raced through my mind.

What if it doesn't work out? What if I care about him more than he cares about me? What if he leaves? What if I let him in just to get my heart broken?

I was pretty certain that at some point between fudge covered Oreo cookies and cat sweaters I'd fallen in love with Reid. I'd never been in love before, so it wasn't like I had a frame of reference. Not to mention how confused I was over my feelings, since what I felt wasn't anything like the way falling in love had ever been described to me before. It wasn't like the movies and the books I'd read. Maybe falling in love was different for everybody. Maybe, it was like the snowflake effect and no two people fall in love the same way.

It hurt, like a physical pain in my chest. Whenever I was with him all my emotions felt like they were just under the surface of my skin. It was overwhelming, like sensory overload. I was equal parts ecstatic and terrified, my heart ached and I just wanted to hold on tight forever. If this was love, then I was finally starting to understand the expression crazy in love, because it felt like I was losing my damn mind.

Even when I was upset and giving the girls a recap of our first date I hadn't divulged how he made me feel. I hadn't told them about the connection I'd felt. I hadn't told the girls about the grocery store until I saw Reid again at fight night, and I didn't tell them what he'd whispered in my ear at the diner either. It was as if a part of me knew that the connection we had was ours and no one else's. I didn't want to share every detail, there were some things that I wanted to keep for myself.

I just hoped that finally putting myself out there didn't result in getting squashed, because if the fear of falling in love had be terrifying, I didn't want to know what a hard landing would do to me.

Twenty-Two

Halloween and Harlots

"I changed my mind," I announced, walking into the kitchen where Alex was thumbing through a tattoo magazine.

She didn't look up from the page when she responded, "About what?"

"My costume."

"What's wrong with your costume?"

I huffed in exasperation, "There's going to be a dozen witches and nurses and whatever else can be made slutty by scissors and glitter. I need something different, unique, but still slutty."

"Why does it have to be slutty?" she asked, still not looking up at me.

"Because it's Halloween, the one night of the year where it is perfectly acceptable to look like a total hussy," I said, the 'duh' was silent.

Alex sighed and finally looked up at me, "You do realize that it is..." she trailed off and looked at the clock on the stove, "Three o'clock and you want to completely change your costume for a party that starts in five hours, right?"

"Oh come on, that's plenty of time!"

"You also realize that every Halloween store in town is going to be picked over by the last-minute vultures and the likelihood of you finding anything you actually like is slim to none?"

"When did you become a pessimist?"

"I'm not, I'm a realist. And the reality of the situation is, you're fucked."

"Not if I have my bestest friend in the whole wide world helping me," I sing-songed and threw my best puppy dog face at her imploringly.

She rolled her eyes, trying and failing to hide her amused smile. Alex pretended she didn't like my crazy antics but really, I was a source of entertainment for her. Alex looked me up and down taking in all of my 5'3" wonder.

I knew what she saw; long brown hair, cute face, nice skin, a little extra junk in the every-fucking-where. I was by no means skinny, I liked to think of myself as healthy. Only, my version of healthy meant eating a bag of Cheetos while binge watching Netflix. Definitely not a size 0 like Nova, who would also be at this party, so I had to look awesome. I wasn't fat or anything. No, I just really fucking hated exercising and really liked food. Cheese was probably my favorite food group. That would be why my ass was pushing the limits of the stitching in the size 10 jeans I was sporting. While I may not have been runway model skinny, I made up for it with ample tits and a decent ass. I'd do me.

In the words of my greatest hero of all time Amy Schumer, I'm 160 pounds, and I can catch a dick whenever I want.

"Hey," Alex said interrupting my daydream. "Do you still have that holster from your Han Solo costume a couple years ago?" I could see her eyes starting to twinkle with whatever idea she was coming up with.

The woman was an evil genius when it came to make up, clothes and whatever the fuck other girly shit she did. Don't get me wrong, I loved clothes and make up just as much as the next girl but Alex was in a realm of her own. The woman had a suitcase full of makeup and hair products. She could turn a homeless woman into a runway model in like 35 minutes. There was a definite possibility that she missed her calling as a makeup artist. She was always on point; make up done, perfectly styled hair, impeccably coordinated outfit, everything. Even when she was doing physical labor or after a five-hour session on somebody's back piece she could come out of it looking like she was ready to go to the fucking state dinner.

I had known Alex for a long time and even before all the makeup and the tattoos and the hair dye she was always put together. But things took a more serious turn when her father got deported.

Her parents had come to the United States on work visas before Alex and Javi were born. A few months after Javi shipped out on his first tour and Alex was just starting art school their dad got a DUI and unfortunately that shed light on the fact that he'd overstayed his work visa by about 20 years. Alex's mom, Carmen followed him back to their home town just outside of Guadalajara. Their parents were now living comfortably in Mexico and enjoying their retirement, but something had changed in Alex. Her OCD had grown more obvious, while it wasn't at the *True Life: I have OCD* level, she needed things to be orderly and controlled.

Now, the only time she ever got dirty was when her fiery temper got the best of her and she had to get physical. It wasn't very often, and even less now that we were adults. Usually it was just a lot of bark and less bite but if she had to back it up, she would. I'd seen her throw down with the boys a few times when we were growing up and she was quite the scrapper.

"Yeah, I do. But Han Solo, while way fucking cool, is not really what I'm going for," I replied, wondering where the hell she was going with this. Harrison Ford was a hot piece of ass but gender swapping that particular character was not the kind of sexy I was trying to achieve.

"You're not going to be Han Solo; I just need the belt. I know exactly what you're going to be, and it's sufficiently nerdy enough for your tastes. You're going to love it."

***

The bar was already crowded when we arrived. I scanned the mass of bodies for Reid but I couldn't see him. The entire space had been transformed. Cobwebs were stretched across the ceiling beams, a fog machine and black lights enhanced the spooky feel. These were not cheesy Dollar Store decorations. Skeletons and ghouls were suspended from the ceiling and tangled in a giant spider's web. They looked as if they were hand painted, and while I'd never personally seen a skeleton or a ghoul, they seemed pretty realistic to me. Orange and lime green lights highlighted the bar where the bartenders were dressed up as zombies.

"Hey," A deep voice rumbled in my ear.

Spinning around I came face-to-face with a grinning Reid. Letting my eyes roam freely down his body, I pouted when I noticed he was wearing yellow zip up coveralls that did nothing for his fine ass body and a gas mask on his head. "Who are you supposed to be?" I asked, still frowning. Did he not get the whole sexy Halloween costume thing? I was sincerely hoping that cowboy hat would make a re-appearance. I'd always kind of had this Tristan from Legends of the Falls cowboy fantasy and seeing him in that hat had given me ideas. Filthy, dirty ones.

He looked at me in disbelief, "Are you kidding me? I'm Jesse from *Breaking Bad*."

"Oh. Yeah, I've never seen that show," I replied with a shake of my head and a shrug.

"What?" he whispered. "How have you never seen *Breaking Bad*? It's like the best show ever."

"I'm sure it is," I nodded, humoring him, because everyone knew that *Doctor Who* was the best show ever, duh.

"We're gonna put a pin in this for later. Don't worry, we'll rectify your *Breaking Bad* situation." He gave me a pitying look and a pat on the shoulder before returning my question. "So what are you supposed to be? Carmen Sandiego?"

Looking down at myself I realized I was still wearing my trench coat. I smirked, "No, that would be a good one, but my costume is underneath." Taking my time, I loosened the knot around my waist and let the coat slip off my shoulders slowly. Reid's eyes bulged as my tight tank top, tiny shorts, and gun holster were revealed.

"Sweet baby Jesus," he muttered under his breath. I noticed his eyelids droop a little and his face had slackened as he continued to stare at my body.

"You like?" I asked and cocked an eyebrow.

"How did you know?" he whispered.

"Know what?"

"That I was in love with Laura Croft when I was 12."

I threw my head back and laughed, it was too perfect. Reid startled me as he quickly grabbed my hips and pulled me to him. I let out a gasp and wrapped my arms around his neck.

"You're leaving this on tonight," he grumbled as he buried his face in my neck.

"You like it that much, huh?"

"Mmm hmmm," He murmured. "You're going to make all my prepubescent fantasies come true."

I laughed again, deciding to tease him a bit, I arched my back and pressed my breasts into his chest. The move elicited a growl from him and he pulled me even closer, making sure I felt every inch of is *appreciation* for my costume.

I loved the way his strong arms felt around me, even if the plastic of his coveralls chafed a bit on my bare skin. He pulled back slightly and cupped my face. He didn't say anything though. He just stared into my eyes. Normally eye contact freaked me out, but Reid always made a point to look me in the eye and I was starting to get used to it, at least from him. Once he was satisfied with whatever he was looking for, he tilted his head and gave me a soft and slow kiss. He was deliberate, and when his tongue entered the game, I moaned. Reid was a phenomenal kisser, heavy on the lips, not too much tongue and just enough teeth. He pulled away too soon and I may have let out a whimper at the loss of his warm mouth.

"Here, let me put your coat behind the bar. I want you to meet some people."

218

Reid introduced me to more people than I could remember. There was his barley guy, his hops guy, and his yeast guy, who was a good sport, laughing at all of my inappropriate yeast jokes.

About an hour later Kellen and Knox had joined us and we were all standing around the high-top table in the bar. Alex, Evie and I were keeping up idle chit chat while Knox was trying to get Kellen to be his wingman. Reid was in deep conversation with one of his bartenders when I noticed Nova walk into the room and I was not the only one.

I swear to God every male head turned when she walked through the doors. She was wearing a teensy tiny white shift dress, a halo and wings. The dress that would've been acceptable on anybody else, was obscenely short on her tall frame, falling high on her thighs. One wrong move and her cooch would be out for the whole world to see. White stilettos adorned her feet making her legs look even longer. Pfft, like she needed it. The girl was a walking talking wet dream wearing virginal white with her light pink lips turned into a sweet smile. She was even wearing glitter eye shadow, which was completely unfair because no one looked good in glitter eye shadow, but this woman somehow managed to pull it off. The crowd parted like the Red Sea as she walked through and headed straight towards us.

"Hey Briar," she said excitedly and gave me a quick hug. I was a little caught off guard but I returned the hug somewhat awkwardly. Reid ended his conversation and turned around, surprised to see Nova standing right next me.

"Nova, hey," he said, leaning in to give her a quick kiss on the cheek and a light hug. Nope, that didn't bother me at all. Just two old friends who used to bone saying 'hello' to each other. How could that possibly put me in a foul mood? It wasn't like we were in an Adele song or anything, sometimes hello just meant hello.

"So glad you could make it," he said.

Reid started to introduce her to everyone at our table when Knox suddenly got up from his stool and walked around to our side of the table squeezing himself right in between me and Nova. He slung an arm over her shoulder and gave her a full toothed smile. I swear to Christ I saw his teeth ding like a fucking Crest commercial.

"Well, hello there," he said looking down at her. She blushed and smiled shyly back up at him. "My name's Knox, let me buy you a drink." She nodded her head and let him lead her over to the bar. Alex, Evie and I shared a look and my brother laughed.

"Typical Knox," Kellen muttered and downed his beer.

"Wow," Nova said addressing Reid when they got back to the table. "This place is amazing. I love what you've done with it."

"Thanks," Reid said, uncharacteristically bashful.

"Honestly, when you told everybody that you were going to go to Portland and open a brewery everybody thought you were crazy but you did it and it's amazing. I'm so happy for you."

I looked at Reid, confused at Nova's words. Open a brewery? I thought he just worked here. Did he actually own the place?

Noticing my confused and slightly pissed off look Reid bent down, whispering in my ear, "I'll explain everything later, I promise." His pleading tone placated my anger just a little bit and I decided to tamp it down and wait for him to explain what the hell was going on and why Nova knew more about him than I did. I quirked an eyebrow and gave him my best you got some 'splaining to do look. I didn't want to make a scene in front of everyone, and I also didn't want to admit to the table that I hadn't known my boyfriend owned a business.

Alex broke the awkward silence, "So Nova, you're new to town?" I had to give her props, the girl was good at small talk. She could ease the awkward in almost any situation, something that was not my strong suit. I guess being a tattoo artist was kind of like being a hairdresser or bartender, you tended to develop a good bedside manner, given that there wasn't much else to do when you're sitting in a chair for hours on end.

"What do you do?" Alex asked. I had spaced out on the conversation but I must not have missed much since we were still on the basic get to know you questions.

"I work for my family's property management company. We just opened an office here in Portland and I am heading up the advertising and marketing division," she replied, looking shyly down at the cocktail napkin she was nervously twisting in her hands.

This is just fanfuckingtastic. She's drop dead gorgeous, successful, and humble. Nova 3, Briar zip.

I zoned out trying to find a flaw on this woman but I couldn't find anything. She was practically perfect. How could that possibly be? As much as I wanted to hate her, from what I could tell she seemed genuine, which kind of made me want to puke. How could I possibly compete with the perfect ex-girlfriend? They were high school sweethearts for Christ sake.

"Earth to Briar," Alex waived her hand in my face.

"Oh, huh?" I asked, wondering how many times they'd called my name while I was lost in thought.

"Nova was just telling us about how they have an HR position open at her office. I was telling her that you have a business degree with a minor in human resource management."

"Yeah, I do," I said turning my attention to Ms. America across the table.

"Really? Oh, my God, we have interviewed so many people and no one is working out. This one guy's hands were so sweaty my boss had to go wash his hands after the meeting. Don't get me wrong, he was a nice guy but it just wasn't the right fit."

"Oh, do you do the hiring there?" I asked. It seemed kind of odd that the head of advertising and marketing would be in an interview for HR.

"Not typically, but we needed an extra person on the panel interview so they brought me in. I get to give my input on the interview but I don't actually make the hiring decision."

"Oh," I said, why did I keep saying oh? I probably sounded like a moron.

"If you want to send me your resume I'd be happy to give it to the hiring manager," she offered.

"Wow, yeah that would be fantastic, thank you." Another point for Nova. Who named their kid Nova anyway? I was well aware that I'd hit the bottom of the insult barrel, but it was still a stupid name.

"Here's my business card. Just email me your resume and I'll forward it to him." I took the card and smiled at her. She didn't need to know that I was trying my damnedest to find a flaw, for all I knew she was doing the same to me, although she would have a lot more to work with.

The rest of the night went off without a hitch. There was a costume contest followed by karaoke and shuffleboard. It was even fun watching Nova repeatedly shoot down Knox. He eventually got the hint and moved on to some harlot dressed as the devil that had been eyeing him across the bar. As the night wound down, the crowd started to disperse and Nova said her goodbyes giving me a hug and reminding me to send her my resume. I thanked her again and waved goodbye.

Twenty - Three

Bad Grandpa

"Why didn't you tell me?" I asked softly as we drove back to Reid's house after the party.

He groaned, scrubbing a hand down his face, "I know, I'm sorry. I just—It didn't seem like that big of a deal."

I was hurt. Why hadn't he trusted me enough to tell me if it wasn't that big of a deal? I just didn't understand. I stayed silent, waiting for him to continue.

"I guess it just didn't come up," he hedged.

"You're joking, right? It didn't come up? How about when you showed me the freaking brewery on our first date? Why didn't you tell me then?" My hurt having morphed into anger with each question.

"Because I wasn't ready to get into it," he said and I could hear the honesty in his voice.

"There's a lot more to it than the fact that I own a brewery. There's a lot of stuff that went on in order for me to get there and I just wasn't ready to tell you about it yet."

"So all that talk about getting to know each other and getting to know the real us was all bullshit?" I asked, angrily.

"God, no Briar, it's not like that at all. By the time I felt like I was ready to tell you about all that shit, I just didn't know how to bring it up again."

"Okay, so the subject's open now, try me." I understood where he was coming from, but I wasn't letting him off the hook. This was his opportunity to explain things so we could move on but it didn't change the fact that I was upset he hadn't wanted to share his past with me.

"It's a long story," he sighed.

"That's okay, we've got all night." There was more than a hint of aggression in my voice. I wanted to know why Nova knew more about him than I did. Despite her sweet disposition, I couldn't shake the jealousy I felt towards the woman. There was just something about her that rubbed me the wrong way. Maybe it was the fact that she and Reid shared a history, or maybe I just didn't want to accept that Reid could have been with someone that was my complete opposite and still want me like I wanted him.

"My parents are wealthy. Well, actually, my grandfather is wealthy and my dad took over the family business when he retired. You have to understand; my parents are nothing like me. They're obsessed with image and money. You know that saying 'keeping up with the Jones''? Yeah, my parents consider it their mission in life to maintain their position on the top of the social ladder."

"Okay, so your parents are stuck up, so what?"

"It's more than that. My mother cares more about what the women in the Rotary think than the happiness of her children. Who does that? What mother is that selfish?" he asked, anger causing his voice to rise.

"What do you mean?" I asked. I could tell there was more to the story than he was letting on.

"When my sister Lana was 18 right before she left for college, she sat us all down and told us she was gay. She was terrified, crying and shaking so hard you'd think she was telling us she murdered someone, not just that she liked girls. My dad looked straight through her for a solid minute, then he got up and told my mother to 'handle it' before he left the room. He completely checked out of the conversation, like he couldn't be bothered. My mom, on the other hand, went ballistic, going on and on about what Julie Perkins and Sasha Marshall would say. She was awful to my sister, telling her no daughter of hers would be a dyke and she better keep her mouth shut. I had never realized how little my mother actually cared about us until that moment."

"I'm so sorry," I said softly, but the words

felt meaningless in the light of his confession. My dad had been an asshole the past few years but he and my mother had always loved my brother and I unconditionally. I couldn't imagine what it must have felt like to grow up like Reid and his sister had.

"Lana let her go on like that for an hour, berating her and calling her ugly names. I wish I could tell you that I'd stood up to my mom and defended my sister, but I didn't. I just sat there like an asshole and listened to her destroy my sister until finally she took off in tears. She stayed with a friend for a few days then drove herself to college. It took a long time for me to forgive myself for not being a better brother and letting her go through that alone."

"How old were you?" I asked, my heart breaking for him. At his core, Reid was the best kind of man. He was thoughtful and accepting of everyone he met. I could only imagine how much it tore him up to think he hadn't been there for his sister in her time of need.

"I was 16. I knew better though. We texted and talked on the phone, but my parents didn't even attempt to contact her. It was like they'd just decided it was easier to cast her aside since she didn't fit into their mold instead of loving her like a family should. Up until that point I'd worked really hard to meet my parents' expectations and be who they'd wanted me to be. I was a spoiled little punk. But after seeing how they'd treated my sister so callously I couldn't do it. I started acting out, tagging, stealing shit just because. Basically, just trying to be the biggest asshole I could in an effort to get back at them. My parents ignored my behavior and just kept on with their parties and weekends at the country club. At least until I got caught and they couldn't ignore me anymore. The judge was lenient but she still scared the crap out of me. So, I got back on the band wagon and started playing by their rules again, but it wasn't the same. It was as if the veil had been drawn back and I could finally see my parents for what they were, cruel and self-absorbed. I did my community service, finished high school, and went off to college like I was supposed to," he said sounding defeated as we pulled into the driveway of a small two story house.

I'd never been to Reid's house before, but now didn't seem like the time to comment on his home. Reid turned off the truck and we sat in silence for a minute before I spoke, "What about your sister?"

"She came back for Christmas every year but it was a total shitshow. My parents doted on her and made sure to praise her academic achievements whenever anyone was in earshot but as soon as the audience was gone they barely even looked at her. Lana put on a brave face, playing the part of the perfect daughter when required, but I knew it was eating her alive. It went on for years, but she just took their abuse. I hated that my sister had built this wall to shield herself from the people that were supposed to be protecting *her*. We fell into this weird Stepford routine, my sister and I letting our parents pull the strings for years."

"What changed?" I asked, blowing on my cold hands. Since he'd turned off the truck the temperature in the cab had dropped significantly. Late October in Portland was no joke.

Seeing my discomfort, Reid climbed out of the truck and motioned for me to follow him. It was an old craftsman style home, and if it was possible, the inside of the house was colder than it had been outside. He flicked on the hall light as soon as we walked in. The house was clearly a fixer upper but from what I could tell the woodwork looked original. My brother had bought a similar style home a year ago and was in the process of a full restoration.

To the left was a set of French doors which led to the living room. "Here, take this and have a seat, I'll start a fire," Reid said handing me a blanket off the back of the couch. I took it and snuggled into the supple brown leather couch, inhaling as I tightened the blanket around my shoulders. It smelled like Reid, something woodsy that I'd come to learn was hops and barley, mixed with the faint smell of acrylic paint. The combination didn't sound like it would smell good but it did, it was comforting because it was all Reid. No one else in the world smelled quite like he did after a day at work and an afternoon at the volunteer center.

My anger with him had subsided sometime during the drive. I just wanted him to tell me the rest of the story, but I knew I needed to wait until he was ready to finish. Reid made quick work of the fire, but instead of coming to sit with me he walked out of the room. I didn't have time to wonder what he was doing because he returned a minute later with a beer in each hand. Passing one to me he asked, "Where were we?"

"What happened to get you guys out of the Stepford routine?"

"Right," he said, sighing heavily. "They didn't show up to her graduation. Lana came up to me after the ceremony and looked at me with these sad eyes that just broke me. She'd known that they weren't going to come, but she'd let a little part of herself hope, and they'd crushed it. Something in me snapped. I was furious. I'd always been an easygoing person but I couldn't take it anymore. I hated my parents in that moment."

"I can't believe they didn't show up," I whispered. "What did you do?"

"I called my dad, told him he was a piece of shit and went out and got drunk with my sister and her girlfriend."

I laughed, "Seriously?"

Reid nodded, chuckling to himself, "Yeah. They were planning a backpacking trip across Europe with some of their friends so I decided to join them. College wasn't for me. I'd tried it for two years and I hated it. I put all my shit in storage, grabbed my passport and every last dime from my savings and left it all behind."

"That's amazing."

"I only got as far as Germany though, I met Brady, the owner of this small brewery on my second night in the country. We hit it off and he offered me a job, I needed the money so I wasn't going to argue but I never planned on staying more than a week or two."

"You told me about him. He taught you how to make beer, right?"

"Yeah, he taught me everything. I worked my ass off and before I knew it I'd been living and working in Germany for a year. It was an awesome experience, but I had to go home eventually. When I got back to Bend, I went straight to my dad and asked him for a loan to start up my own brewery."

"You did?" I asked, shocked.

"I did, and he laughed in my face. Completely shut me down and belittled the business plan I'd drafted up."

"So, what did you do?"

"Well, I told you before that my Grandfather was the rich one, right? I asked him," he shrugged.

"Just like that?" I asked.

"Just like that. He asked me if it was my passion. I told him yes and he wrote me a check on the spot. Told me not to fuck it up and sent me on my way with a pat on the back."

"Your Grandfather told you not to fuck it up?" I asked incredulously.

"My Grandfather is nothing like my dad. In

fact, he kind of hates how my dad turned out. He was a self-made man. No one believed in him when he had a crazy idea to open a ski lodge. Now he's sitting on a fat pile of cash with his name attached to one of this biggest lodges in the country and a half a dozen shops and restaurants. He practically owns the mountain. I honestly think he was so quick to write the check because he knew it would piss my dad off. He believed in me when no one else would and that's how Bearded Jack's started."

"Wow, that's crazy. Do you and your sister talk to your parents at all?"

"Not much. Lana and I try to make Christmas every year but it's still strained. Lana's almost thirty. She's been out for over a decade but because my parents refuse to acknowledge it, she still has to pretend she's in the closet whenever she goes out there. It's fucked up. She shouldn't have to live like that. The only reason we keep making the trip is to see our grandfather, otherwise we wouldn't bother."

"Does your grandfather know that your sister's a lesbian?" I asked, there was probably a subtle way to ask but I was curious and subtlety had never been my strong suit.

Reid barked out a laugh, "Oh he knows. He overheard my sister and I talking about a new girlfriend she had a few years ago. God, Lana had been terrified. He just slapped her on the back and told her he was just glad she wasn't going to turn up pregnant out of wedlock."

"What? Are you serious?"

"Yeah, but it gets better. He was pissed when he found out what mom and dad were doing to her, so he would make offhanded comments during my parents' parties. The first time he asked my sister across the dinner table if she'd seen the latest episode of *Ellen* I almost choked on a piece of steak."

"Go grandpa!" I said, impressed that despite his parents' feelings, Reid's grandfather seemed to care more about his grandchildren than who they fell in love with.

"Yeah, he's a good person. So, what's your story? I know your parents are divorced, but something tells me there's more to it than you've let on."

"What are you, clairvoyant now?" I complained, but to be truthful, I was kind of relieved he'd asked. I'd been wanting to broach the subject of Thanksgiving for a while, but I didn't know how to approach it and this topic would provide the bridge I needed.

"Yes, I come from a broken home," I started, adding just enough dramatic heartbreak to my voice to make him laugh. Humor was my way to negate the seriousness of a situation. If shit was getting too deep, you could bet I'd crack an inappropriate joke to break through the feels. I realized that my defense mechanism was a sign of emotional immaturity, but fuck it, I was still young.

"Come on," Reid encouraged, putting his

arm around my shoulders and cuddling me close. In our position on the couch I didn't have to look at him while I told my story, which made it easier somehow.

"My parents were married for 25 years. One day, during my Christmas break from college, my dad gathered my brother and I in the living room and told us that he and mom were getting a divorce. He said he'd fallen out of love with her and needed to move on. That was it. No fanfare, no tears from him, although there were plenty from my mother. He said he still cared for our mom but he just wasn't in love with her anymore and it wasn't fair to her to keep living like he was. It wasn't just sudden, it was cold. I haven't actually spoken to him since, and that was five years ago. Mom invited him to my graduation, but I refused to speak to him. He's not worth my time."

"I hate to ask, but was he seeing someone else?" Reid asked gently.

"That's probably the most fucked up part, he wasn't cheating. In fact, according to my brother he hasn't had any serious girlfriends or anything since they split five years ago. It doesn't make any sense to me. How do you fall out of love with someone after all those years?"

"I don't know," Reid said softly, hooking a finger under my chin and guiding my face so I was looking up at him. His eyes bore into mine, the intensity of his gaze making me uneasy. "I can't imagine falling out of love," he whispered before sweeping a soft kiss across my lips.

Whoa Nelly! Fire down below!

Reid pulled away before things could get too heated. "What happened next?"

"My mom was heartbroken, a complete mess. I offered to come home and take care of her, but she wouldn't have it. She told me that she was a big girl and that she would figure it out on her own. I hadn't really believed it. She'd been completely blindsided by my dad's sudden change of heart. He'd been her world. For over half of her life she'd loved him and he threw it all away, for nothing. That's what pissed me off the most, there was no reason. No tangible cause for his sudden unhappiness. They didn't fight, at least not more than any other married couple. They had date night every Friday since before I can remember. They had their own hobbies and interests but they kept their traditions together, too. They did everything right, all the things that are supposed to foster a happy marriage, and it still wasn't enough."

"I could tell she was spiraling, every time I called her I could practically hear the depression in her voice. I started driving up from school unannounced to check on her. The summer before my senior year in college, I came home to find her passed out on the couch at noon on a Tuesday, with several empty bottles of wine surrounding her. It had been six months since my dad had moved out and she wasn't getting better with time; she was getting worse."

"Did she work?"

"She's an elementary school teacher, so she has summers off. I think that's the only reason she let herself go that far, she didn't have anything else to do but sit at home and think about shit."

My mother and I were similar in that respect. If I was left to my own devices after a situation like that, I'd have fallen apart as well.

"So, I called my Aunt Cheryl, because she was the only family my mom had, and asked for help. She came down from Seattle and stayed with my mom for a few weeks. They took a couple of trips, and by the time school started in the fall my mom was almost back to her normal self."

"What about your brother? Where was he?"

"My brother was at the fire department academy at the time, he had his own shit to worry about. He still checked on Mom when he could, but I don't think he ever knew how bad it got. I was scared she wasn't going to be able to pull herself out of it. I still don't know how my aunt got through to her, but I'm thankful she did. There's nothing more terrifying than watching someone you love slowly destroy themselves and not being able to do anything about it."

"Yeah, I know what you mean. Depression is a scary thing," Reid replied. There was a pain in his voice that made me wonder if things with his sister had been worse than he'd let on.

Instead of pushing him on his cryptic comment, I snuggled closer and wrapped an arm around his middle, throwing a leg over his for good measure. "Okay, enough with the serious shit for one night."

"Agreed," he chuckled, laying a hand on my hip. "Didn't you promise to fulfill my teenage dreams?"

"Hmm, I don't remember making this promise you speak of," I teased.

"Yes, you promised all sorts of dirty and depraved things. Don't worry, I'm more than happy to remind you."

"I'm sure," I said, sitting up a bit. I'm not sure how he'd managed to turn me on just a few minutes after such a serious conversation, but I wasn't about to complain. There was something about him that made me want him all the time. A little voice in the back of my mind wondered if that would fade over time. If I'd get bored like my dad, or even worse, if he would.

Chucking the blanket, I crawled over and straddled him.

"What are you doing?" Reid asked. His hands instantly came to rest on my outer thighs.

"That conversation is starting to come back to me," I murmured, running my fingers through his hair and gently scratching his scalp with my nails.

"Y-yeah," he stuttered.

"Am I making you nervous?" I asked, giving him my best Jolie-inspired pout. He gripped my thighs tighter but didn't respond. Taking my time, I teased him. My lips grazing across his jaw and down his neck. My hands roaming everywhere they could reach while I shifted my hips and ground against him. His hands stayed on me, travelling up to my hips to help guide my rocking.

I disentangled myself from him and slowly slid down his body letting my hands trail across his shoulders and down his chest, until I rested on my knees between his legs. My hand made fast work of his belt buckle. He'd already shed his costume from the party. I slowly unzipped his pants and he lifted his hips to help me slide them down to mid-thigh. His erection stood tall and rock-hard. I smiled to myself.

I did that.

I glanced up at him through hooded eyes. Reid's nostrils flared and he was breathing more quickly than usual. It wasn't a full-blown pant, but I had plans to change that. I wanted him out of control. I wanted him to lose his mind and not be able to think about anything but me.

Using the very tip of my tongue, I licked up his shaft. Just barely touching and teasing him. Reaching the top, I flicked the silver ball with my tongue, causing him to inhale sharply. I couldn't help myself, I grinned. Starting the trail back down to repeat the process. I took my time teasing him and playing with him, my hands firmly placed on his thighs. I didn't want to give him everything. Just enough to tease, just enough to drive him wild.

Finally, I took his crown into my mouth, sucking hard. I could hear the hitch in his breath as I opened my mouth wider and took him in further. I kept bouncing up-and-down until the head of his cock hit the back of my throat, causing my gag reflex to kick in. I choked a little and felt his dick swell in my mouth. He got harder, if that was even possible, and his hips jerked involuntarily. His hands were balled into fists at his side. I felt a surge of heat between my legs and my pussy tightened.

That was hot.

I pulled up again and plunged back down, loving the way he reacted every time he hit the back of my throat. But my little game was short-lived because Reid grabbed me by the arms and hauled me up, quickly pinning me to the couch on my back. The move was so sudden I didn't have time to react before his mouth slammed down mine.

He kissed me hard and desperately. His tongue plunging into my mouth and swirling with my own. His hands frantically searched for the clasps to unhook the gun harness that was part of my costume. When he couldn't get it undone he sat up on his knees and quickly discarded the harness as well as my shorts and lacy thong. He crashed back down on top of me hitching an arm under one of my knees before he positioned himself and slammed into me.

All the air left my lungs in a whoosh followed by a deep gasp when he started to move.

There was no gentleness in the way he took me. The realization that I'd succeeded in my attempts to make him lose control had me panting and writhing beneath him. Reid's heated touch left a scorched path across my skin. He bit and sucked at my neck while my nails left trails down his back.

I was so worked up from before, that my orgasm started to build quickly and I was blindsided with its intensity. My climax roared through my body, causing my nails to dig deeper into Reid's back, which in turn sent him over the edge. His entire body went ridged, and he groaned into my ear as his release hit him.

Reid quickly flipped us around so that he was laying on his back and my languid body was draped on top of him on the couch. We were both sweaty and panting, but neither of us pulled apart. I rested my head on his chest and listened to the thump, thump, thump of his heart. It was a perfect moment. Skin to skin, in a relaxed heap with Reid playing with my hair. If I had to imagine what heaven was like, this would be it.

Twenty-Four

Power Panties and Pissing Matches

Nova had made good on her promise, and after a brief phone screening with the head of HR, Mr. Herman. I had an interview for the following Wednesday. According to Mr. Herman, Marshall Realty owned several properties in the Portland Metro area which were formerly managed by the Bend office. Since they planned on expanding, they transferred those properties over to the new office in Portland. Mr. Herman had recently relocated from Bend to head up the HR department and was looking for an HR specialist to work under him.

I walked into to the interview with a confidence only power panties could supply. You know what I'm talking about, when your bra and underwear match you just feel more put together.

Add a garter belt and you have power panties. There's something empowering about knowing you've got it going on underneath your clothes, you're ready for anything at the drop of a hat. You know how your mother always told you to wear clean underwear because if you ever got in a car accident and they had to cut off your clothes, you don't want to get caught with nasty period panties? Gross, right? Well if you get into an accident while wearing power panties you're likely to get a date with the hot EMT. See my point?

Armed with my undergarment arsenal and charming disposition, I knocked it out of the park. I was pleasant and professional. I gave thoughtful responses to the questions all thanks to Alex and Evie who helped me refine some of the answers. The following day I got a call back from Mr. Herman offering me the job. It paid way better than the temp agency I was currently working for and I told him I could be available to start the following Monday. I know you're always supposed to give a two weeks' notice but it was a temp agency so who the fuck really cares, right?

After a week of training, I was let loose on my own to wreak havoc. In actuality, as the new specialist I was basically Mr. Herman's bitch. Not that he treated me badly or anything but I was a glorified assistant nonetheless. At least now I was in the right department, instead of playing personal gimp to the wicked witch of advertising. This job had potential for growth, which was what I was looking for.

Mr. Herman, who had repeatedly asked me to call him by his first name Geoffrey, which I refused, because I really couldn't say it with a straight face. It was pronounced Joff-ray, which is just ridiculous for a squat, round man that tended to pit-out whenever he walked more than twenty feet. It wasn't all making copies and filing though, Mr. Herman actually gave me the opportunity to do some real HR stuff. I just didn't know at the time that it was a total bait and switch.

He started out by asking if I wanted to handle a project on my own, really show the company what I could do. He even went as far as to say the request for the project had come straight from the CEO and he would be sure to tell him what a great job I had done. Of course, I jumped at the opportunity. Umm, hello? Getting to show what I'm made of at a new job right out of the gate? Bring it on.

I soon realized the error of my ways when I was handed a stack of employee files taller than me. My big shinny project? I was to interview every employee and do a pulse check on employee satisfaction. Apparently, the CEO had read about it in a business journal and since happy employees are productive employees...you get the picture.

It was my fifth day in a row of being confined to a tiny eight by ten office for eight hours a day listening to employees complain. I didn't think they could have that much to bitch about considering the office had just opened four months ago. Wrong. At least half of the employees relocated from Bend and the other half had years of experience in the industry, and people that work in offices have so much to bitch about.

Who knew that taking the last of the coffee without making a new pot was a mortal sin? Well, Mina in accounting sure thought so. From what I'd heard, she was a monster. When I was talking to Kyle from marketing he confided in me that once he'd taken the last of the coffee and didn't make a new pot because it was the afternoon and he figured it would go to waste.

Apparently, as he was walking back to his desk she called over the cubicle wall to him in a creepy voice, saying she would cut him if he didn't go back and make the pot of coffee. I thought it was kind of funny until he told me when he went over to apologize after making the fresh pot, one of their co-workers told him she'd been out sick all day. He told me he was so scared that a little pee came out. I hadn't met with her yet but I kind of wanted to shake her hand. The coffee keeper and I could totally trade notes.

I was sitting in my little office, daydreaming about the hazelnut latte I was going to get on my break, while listening to Barb from payroll prattle on. She held nothing back, as she continued to bitch about Jerry in her department.

"He's disgusting," she exclaimed in a nasally voice. Three minutes into talking to this woman and I could already tell that when she got excited only dogs could hear her. For such a large woman, she had a very high-pitched, squeaky voice.

"Barb, why don't you tell me what exactly it is that's bothering you?" I asked calmly, trying to speed things up because her bitching was wasting my goddamn time. I hadn't had nearly enough coffee and her voice was giving me a migraine.

"He clipped his nails at his desk!" she shouted, completely unaware of the volume of her voice or the fact that the walls were so thin that everyone in the office could probably hear her.

"Okay," I said and scribbled something on my notepad. I had to at least pretend to care because this woman was bat shit crazy, and I did not need her setting her beady little eyes on me. It's not like I could really do anything about the stuff she was bitching about.

Well, maybe the fingernail clipping.

"He coughs and hacks all day, it's gross," she continued. "Don't get me started on his coffee cups! He has a half dozen half empty cups on his desk that are at different stages of growing mold!"

I had to stifle a laugh because Jerry was a lot like me in the sense that I didn't usually rush to wash out my coffee cups.

You've got to be kidding me, what were we coming to?

She had nothing better to do than bitch about multiple coffee cups on someone else's desk? Why did she care that much?

"And he took a call that was for me when I was sitting right there!"

"Have you brought any of this to your manager's attention?" I asked sweetly.

"Yes, but she keeps telling me to mind my own business and just keep my head down and work and that's just not okay!" she shrieked, her voice climbing another octave. "This is a hostile work environment!"

Son of a bitch.

She'd brought out the big guns. This woman just earned a spot on my permanent shit list. Anyone who's ever been in HR knows when someone brings up a red flag phrase like 'hostile work environment', it's the equivalent of a ticking time bomb. So now I would have the joy of making sure every one of her complaints was documented and addressed by management. There was no room for error, because people that use phrases like that, are the people that sue. Whether it's justified or not, they get paid.

Fucking whore.

***

An hour later I was still typing up my notes from my meeting with Beast-mode Bitch Barb, when there was a knock at my door, again. I must've made an impression because everyone and their fucking mother had been dropping by my office to complain about the pettiest of shit. Frustrated, I looked up, readying my pleasant and professional 'fuck off' face, only to see Reid leaning casually against the doorframe.

I started to salivate, not at Reid, although he was plenty drool worthy, but at the steaming cup of coffee he held in his hand. He pushed off the door and strolled into my office.

"I know it's been a rough week, thought you might need an afternoon pick-me-up," he said, but I was focused on the glorious smell of espresso and foamed milk.

Reaching both hands out I made a grabbing motion and whimpered, I couldn't form words yet, I needed caffeine first. Reid laughed and handed the coffee over, after just a few months of dating he knew me pretty well. The thought caught me off guard as I took the offering and savored it. If I was being honest with myself, it kind of freaked me out.

Our relationship had progressed easily and it felt natural. I wanted to be with him all the time, and he seemed to feel the same way about me, but I was still worried he was going to suddenly think I was being clingy or something. I hated that quality in men.

If any of my past boyfriends had shown up at my job unannounced I would have had a total bitch fit about boundaries, but as I looked at Reid over the top of my red paper cup the only thing I felt was appreciation. He was thoughtful and kind, qualities that while I'd always thought were important, had never been as sexy as they were on the guy standing in front of me.

It's a funny thing when you realize you are more turned on by someone's personality than their looks. Reid was hot, no doubt about that and hung like a fucking horse but I found myself getting more hot and bothered by the fact that he had heard me when I was venting about what a rough week I'd had. He'd been thinking about me today and took action to make my day just a little bit better. That was a man. That was the definition of sexy.

"What?" he asked, at my perusal.

"Just thinking about how much I want to jump you right now," I stated, never taking my eyes off of his.

Reid chuckled uncomfortably and looked back through the open door to make sure no one had heard me. When he looked back my way, I noticed his face was starting to flush, pink creeping up his neck. I loved how easily I made him blush.

"Thank you for the coffee, I appreciate it," I said making my way over to him, I lifted up on my toes and kissed his cheek sweetly. "I'll show you how much tonight," I whispered in his ear before pulling back and taking a step away, for professional appearances of course. It's not as though shutting the door and playing a game of hide the salami was really a possibility at the moment. No, the walls were far too thin for that.

"My place or yours?" he asked, his voice barely rumbling above a whisper.

"Yours, I'm feeling kind of loud today," I said, smirking as his blush deepened. He really was too easy. "Come on, I'll walk you out."

We passed by Nova's office on our way out, her office door was shut and she appeared to be on a conference call. She looked surprised when she saw Reid through the glass panel next to her door. He waived and a bright smile took over her face as she started to wave back, but it fell suddenly as I came into view. She tried to cover up the flub by waiving excitedly at me and pointing to her phone to indicate she was on a call, but there was something forced about it.

What was that?

To anyone else it would have been nothing, a non-event, but something in my gut had told me from the beginning that this girl was just too nice to be real.

"You didn't have to walk me all the way to my car," Reid said as we reached his truck.

Yes, I did, I thought to myself. The windows in Nova's office faced the parking lot, and as immature as it was I wanted her to see us together. I told myself it wasn't petty; it was a test. If she acted differently towards me after this then it would confirm my suspicions about her, if not then maybe she really was a nice person.

Yeah, fucking right.

"But I can't do this in the office," I said, wrapping my arms around his neck and stretching up for a kiss. Reid's hands slipped around my waist to settle on the small of my back as he pulled me closer. I was out of breath by the time we pulled apart, I hadn't planned for things to get that intense but it seemed impossible not to get carried away every time Reid's lips touched mine.

"I'll see you tonight," I said softly.

I was in a daze of sorts as I walked back into the office, my heart was still pounding and my stomach was full of butterflies. It was a new and odd experience for me, I was actually giddy. My elation was short lived, because when I walked by Nova's office and waved, she gave me a wide and extremely fake smile.

Interesting.

Nova waltzed into my office an hour later, setting off all kinds of alarm bells in my head.

"I was surprised to see Reid here," Nova said, settling herself into one of the chairs on the opposite side of my desk.

Whoa, way to get right to the point.

"Yeah, he was just bringing me coffee," I answered, not giving anything away. If she wanted more she was going to have to ask for it.

"I didn't realize you were together..." she trailed off.

"Yeah, we've been dating for a few months, I thought you knew," I said with mock innocence but my eyes were focused solely on the woman in front of me. I saw her jaw clench when I said 'dating', yeah she didn't like that one bit.

She cleared her throat and stood up. "I guess I just assumed you weren't, you're not his usual type, no offense or anything. He just usually goes for a...*different* kind of woman." The fake concern in her voice making my stomach churn.

Trying to play on my insecurities? Not today, bitch.

"Yeah, I know. He's not my normal type either but he was just so *persistent* when he was pursuing me so I gave him a shot. I'm glad I did, he's an amazing boyfriend."

Take that you dirty snatch!

"Good, I'm glad for you two. Reid's one of the good ones, don't let him get away," she said, trying way too hard to be overly friendly.

"Don't worry, only and idiot would let a guy like Reid get away."

Suck it, skank.

She gave me a curt smile and left without so much as a goodbye. I'd have to keep my eyes on her, because if I'd learned anything in high school it was that the sweetest girls could be the nastiest bitches. If she decided she was going to try and make a move on Reid she'd be in for a rude awakening because I wasn't afraid to play dirty.

Twenty-Five

Festivities and Fuckwads

I groaned as I fumbled for my phone, slapping at the screen until the alarm shut the hell off.

"Jesus," Reid grumbled next to me, "It sounds like the zombie apocalypse." He was, of course, referring to the annoying siren alarm on my phone.

While it was the most obnoxious sound ever, it was the only thing that had any chance of waking my ass up at 4 o'clock in the morning. Jesus Christ, why did I decide to do Thanksgiving at my house this year? No one in their right mind should be up at 4 o'clock when they don't have to work.

Heaving myself out of bed I padded down the hall into the kitchen. First order of business was coffee. I circumvented the giant 26-pound turkey in my sink in order to fill up the coffee pot. Evie tried to get us to buy one of those individual cup coffee machines but I wasn't having it. I needed an entire pot at my disposal at all times I was not going to wait for that individual cup bullshit. Not to mention those things made weak ass coffee, I liked my brew strong.

Watching the coffee percolate, I wondered where the hell the other bitches were. We'd all agreed to get up at the butt crack of dawn to start prep for Thanksgiving dinner but I must've woken up in an alternate universe, because for some ungodly reason I was the only one up.

Stomping down the hall I swung open the door to Alex's room and switched on the light. "Wake up, cunt cake!" I shouted as I burst into her room, only to find her already dressed and pulling her hair up into a messy bun.

"Pipe down, princess. It's too early for that level of enthusiasm," she rasped as she turned from the mirror on her vanity and shuffled towards me.

"You're no fun," I grumbled and headed towards Evie's room.

"Rise and shine, bitch!" I announced as I flung Evie's door open in much the same fashion as I had Alex's.

"I hate you," she grumbled.

"Dude, you promised."

"Fine! Just stop fucking screaming," she complained, pushing herself up she glared at me through a mess of blonde tangles.

I backed out of the room slowly, because it was all fun and games until Evie got pissed, then you better watch your back. Polly Anna could get brutal as fuck.

I walked into the kitchen to find Alex already pouring a cup of coffee and Evie hot on my heels.

"Now who's going to get all the icky stuff out of the turkey?" I asked, "Because it sure as hell isn't going to be me."

All three of us stood in front of the sink staring at the giant bird.

"Not it!" called Evie, touching her nose with her forefinger to emphasis her point.

"Don't look at me, I'm not touching that thing!" Alex said, her face contorted in disgust.

"I'll do it." Reid grumbled as he walked into the kitchen, "Out of my way."

"Captain save-a-ho to the rescue!" I shouted as he rolled up his sleeves and moved towards the bird.

Once Reid successfully de-icky-fied the turkey, we began to chop and stuff, and stir and chop some more, and mix, and did I mention chop? We worked for the rest of the morning and into the afternoon until the smell of Thanksgiving dinner filled the house.

Normally when I cooked it was a solitary activity, I liked to let my mind wander and mull over whatever was bothering me. It was like my own form of therapy, if I was upset or frustrated I could chop and pound out my emotions and when I finished, I had an awesome meal to enjoy and more often than not a solution to my problems.

I used the quiet time while I cooked dinner to reflect on the past week and a half. After coffee-gate as I'd grown accustom to referring to the incident, Nova had been off. First was that weird pissing match we'd had in my office. Having an entire argument in subtext was exhausting, we both knew what the other meant but we needed to maintain plausible deniability, and since nothing was said outright I couldn't exactly go to Reid and tell him his ex-girlfriend wanted him back.

Then last week I went into her office to drop off some hire paperwork for her newest team member and I noticed a picture that hadn't been there before. Right up front, facing out in clear view of anyone that walked into the office, was a picture of her and Reid. Two older couples who I assumed were their parents flanked them on either side. They were young, probably seventeen in the picture, but that didn't lessen the sting of seeing him with his arms wrapped tight around another woman.

I was surprised at how much the photo had rattled me. She was a part of his past; her family was friends with his family. Even if he wasn't close to them today, what if he wanted to be someday? Would I fit in with my loud mouth and mediocre manners? Would she cause problems if that day ever came? So many questions were spinning in my head and the one person that I wanted to talk them out with, the one person that would understand me was Reid, and he was the one person I couldn't talk to.

The doorbell rang, pulling me from my thoughts. I glanced around the kitchen and into the living room but my brother was nowhere to be found. Instead, I called out to Reid who was sitting on the couch watching football. "Hey babe, can you answer the door? I'm elbow deep in stuffing."

"Got it," he called out and I heard him open the door to greet someone.

"Babe? How domestic," Alex said with a smirk.

"Oh shut up," I said giving a pointed look towards my mother who was sitting on the other side of the island playing on her phone.

"Whatever," she said, returning her attention to the gravy she'd been stirring. I loved my mother, but if she got even the barest hint of 'domesticated' from me and Reid she would be picking out china patterns by Christmas.

"Smells great in here," a voice filtered in and I froze. It was my dad. I'd know that voice anywhere. I knew he was coming. I had told Kellen that it was okay to invite him after I talked to mom and she had insisted that it wasn't a problem. That didn't change fact that I hadn't actually spoken to him in over five years and now he was here in my house complementing the smells of my cooking. "I brought wine. Where should I put it?" he asked.

I refrained from responding with a 'straight up your ass' and instead nodded my head to the island. "Thanks, you can put it over there." I said crisply and turned my back on him to wash my hands.

"Bill, it's so nice to see you," my mom said, standing up to greet him with a hug.

"Gloria, you look beautiful as always," he said.

I watched them over my shoulder as they exchanged pleasantries. Feeling a twinge in my chest and tears start to prick behind my eyelids, I turned back to the sink. How was she doing this? How were they both pretending everything was okay while I was over here two seconds away from falling apart?

"The place looks great, honey," my dad tried again to engage me.

"It's all Alex. I'm not much of an interior decorator," I bit out. I realized that I was being a dick but I couldn't get myself to let it go.

Just then, I felt two strong arms wrap around my middle and Reid's chest press up against my back. I instantly felt safe. I knew no matter what he had my back, and it felt good that at least one person was in my corner.

He bent down and whispered in my ear, "I know it's a lot, just try and be nice. Act like he's just any other guest, Okay?"

I took a deep breath, covering his arms with my own and leaning back into him. I nodded in agreement, "I'll try."

"It'll all be okay," he said, giving me another squeeze and kissing the top of my head before pulling away.

I focused my attention on cooking as more guests filtered in. Javi, Alex's twin brother showed up donning a six-pack of beer. Jack, Evie's dad was next. He also brought a six-pack of beer. I guess it was some unwritten single guy code.

Knox and his grandmother Betty were the last to arrive. Betty was just about my favorite person on the planet. She was a spitfire, with mop of bright white curls and a knowing twinkle in her eye. You couldn't get anything past the woman, she'd heard and seen it all and she wasn't afraid to let you know it. Her wild stories about living it up as a stewardess in the 60s used to keep me on the edge of my seat for hours when I was younger. I was amazed by her. She'd cut her own path through life in a time when women were expected to fit in a box and be seen, not heard. That was the life I wanted for myself, to have adventures, buck tradition, and be unapologetically me.

When Knox's mom passed away when he was 12 and his dad got sent to prison, he came to live with Nan and, lo and behold, she just happened to live three doors down from us. She had insisted since we were kids that we all call her Nan which we obediently did because you just don't say no to a 70-year-old woman that had no qualms about beating you with a wooden spoon.

"Nan!" I exclaimed, running over to give her a hug.

"Oh, baby girl!" she said, "Look at you. My grandson tells me that you got yourself a new beau." She smirked and gave me a sly, knowing wink.

I laughed, waiving Reid over. "Nan, this is Reid. Reid, this is Nan."

"It's a pleasure to meet you," he said, making a show of bowing and kissing the back of her hand. He was such a suck up. He'd done the same thing to my mother and she'd nearly melted into a puddle on the floor.

"Well, aren't you quite the charmer," Nan pronounced, her other hand finding its way to her chest.

"Stop flirting with my grandmother, you freak!" Knox shouted from behind her, which in turn earned him a slap upside the head from Nan.

Nan made her rounds greeting everybody. She really was the matriarch of the family even if it wasn't really a family. After years of adding people to the mix, we were more like a ragtag group of misfits, but we were her misfits and she wouldn't have it any other way.

"Dinner's about ready," I called out. The guys were in the living room watching a football game but Nan, and my mother were sitting at the island chatting while Alex and I worked. Evie had long since been relieved of her chopping duties and I could hear her screaming at the T.V. about a bad call. Being raised by a single guy had done nothing for Evie's domestic sensibilities. It was best if we limited her participation to prep work.

"I'll set the table, sweetheart," my mother said picking up the large stack of plate's I'd taken down from the cabinet.

"Thanks, Ma."

The role reversal of watching my mother set the table for a meal that I'd prepared was bizarre. The huge farm table was one of the first big purchases I'd made for myself when I got my own place. There was nothing better than having a house full of friends and family to enjoy a meal together. After years at my mother and Nan's apron strings, the one thing that I could do was cook and cook very well. I just had two problems, I couldn't stop eating what I cooked and I hated cleaning. Both of which mostly kept me from the kitchen unless I was entertaining.

***

We said Grace, a requirement of Nan's at every meal. After, I turned to my brother. "Kellen, will you carve the turkey?" I asked and handed him the carving knife and fork.

He gave me a hesitant look out of the corner of his eye, but eventually nodded his head and took the utensils. I didn't specifically mean it to be a dig at my father, but it was a happy after effect. My father had always prided himself in carving the turkey and sitting at the head of the table. It was kind of a big deal to him. By not giving him the opportunity to do so at my house during Thanksgiving was a bit of salt in the wounds.

I was afraid that the dinner conversation would be stilted due to the clear animosity coming from me towards my father, but seeing as everyone knew each other pretty well it went decently. Mom managed get Nan to start talking about her days as a stewardess and within a few minutes everyone was laughing.

Jack, who had been quiet at first, started to open up. He was kind of like Evie in that way. Quiet at first but once you got to know them you couldn't shut them up. Evie and I met on the first day of college orientation when we were assigned as roommates. It wasn't besties at first sight. Evie was quiet and studious, while I was totally there to party. When Thanksgiving break rolled around we reluctantly decided to drive up to Portland together to save on gas. During the drive, Evie had opened up to me a little bit, telling me about how it was just her and her dad and then she revealed the most horrific details about their Thanksgiving tradition. They ate microwave turkey dinners and watched football all day.

At that point our little holiday tradition had already extended to Knox and his grandmother. I insisted that she bring her father to Thanksgiving dinner at our house and refused to take no for an answer. Reluctantly, she agreed and the rest is history.

It also helped that Knox trained at Jack's gym, so he was familiar with Evie's father and easily pulled him into conversation.

To my surprise the only odd one out was Javi. Even though he'd been around longer than Evie or her father, he'd been gone for a long time. I could tell from the way he kept looking around that he was having a hard time finding where he fit in. Alex mentioned it before. She was worried about how he was acclimating to civilian life since he'd gotten home a few weeks ago.

I tried to engage him, "So, Javi, what are you doing now that you're stateside?"

"Don't know yet actually," he said quietly. "I've considered reenlisting, but Alex doesn't want me to go overseas again so I might stick around. I just have to find something to do."

"What branch?" Jack asked. He'd never actually met Javi before. In fact, this was the first holiday Javi had spent with us in almost eight years.

"Marines, Sir," Javi responded.

"Semper Fi," Jack nodded in approval, "I served in the first Gulf War."

Javi perked up at his words, the first sign of the full of life Javi I used to know breaking through his hardened eyes. "Oh yeah? Where were you stationed?"

"Kuwait," Jack responded.

"Me too," Javi said, a hint of a smile playing at the corners of his mouth. "First and third tour."

Jack tipped his chin, "If you need work, I'm always looking for a good conditioning trainer. Do you have any boxing, or mixed martial arts experience?"

"Yeah, I used to box back on the base."

"Good, come down to the gym next week and I'll put you through the paces."

"That'd be great. Thank you, sir." I noticed Alex relax back into her seat, some of the tension draining from her face. She'd been nervous about her twin fitting into civilian life again, but Javi was resilient, he'd figure it out.

"Bill," Nan pipped up, "What have you been doing? It's been a long time." Leave it to Nan to go straight for the jugular. If the subject was taboo or uncomfortable, the older woman was sure to bring it to the front and center. She always said unfinished business was like a cancer, it would eat you alive from the inside out so you better pull on your big girl panties and face the problem head on.

"Yeah," my dad said uncomfortably, "I've just been working. We branched out and opened a new office in Seattle so I've been traveling back-and-forth."

Yes, because the insurance business was all about jet setting.

"Business is good I hope?"

"Yes, ma'am. It is," he said, staring at his mashed potatoes.

"Good, good. What are you up to, Gloria?" I had to stifle a laugh because Nan already knew what my mother had been up to. They still lived three doors down from each other. Nan was not a subtle person. This line of questioning was clearly so my father could hear how fantastic my mother's life was without him.

"Oh things are going great! In fact, I'm planning a trip to Europe this summer when school lets out," she said. My eyes snapped to my mother, this was the first I was hearing about this. She was a teacher at the elementary school we went to as kids. I made a mental note to ask her how the hell she was going to afford a European vacation.

"That's fantastic, Gloria! Do you know where you're going to go?" said Nan.

"Well, my girlfriend and I are going to spend two months traveling. We've got it all mapped out. Ireland, Scotland, England, then off to Germany, France, Spain, and finally ending in Italy. It's a dream come true!" she squeaked excitedly.

"Germany is great, Gloria. I used to live there. If you'd like I'll write down a couple of places you should be sure to check out that aren't exactly in the tourist books," Reid offered.

"That would be lovely. Thank you, Reid." My mother said, blushing. I was beginning to think my mother had a little crush on my boyfriend. I glanced at my father, the corners of his mouth tipped down and I noticed his shoulders had slumped a little more than usual. I continued to watch him as Reid and my mom talked about the wonders of Europe. Once or twice I noticed his eyes dart to her and a look of longing pass over his face before he looked back down at his plate.

Yeah, fuckwad. Look at what you gave up.

"Oh! I almost forgot," Nan interrupted, drawing everyone's attention. "Alex, dear, I was wondering if you'd be available sometime in the next few weeks."

"Sure, what's up?"

"Well, I'd like to get some ink." she said with gusto.

Knox nearly spit out his beer, "You want what, Nan?"

"Isn't that what the kids call it nowadays? I want a tattoo."

"Nan, why now? After all this time?" Knox argued, immediately the table went silent and everyone averted their eyes.

"Are you saying I'm too old?" she asked glaring at Knox with her sharp eyes.

Apparently, Knox had woken up with a fucking death wish. "Nan, this is ridiculous. You're almost eighty!"

"I may be old, but I'm not dead yet, you little shit!" she said, flicking him in the forehead with an arthritic finger.

"Ow! Shit, Nan."

"Don't be such a pansy. I can't believe they let you be a fire fighter with the way you bitch." At that we all erupted in laughter. Nan was one of a kind, that's for sure.

"Do you know what you want?" Alex asked,

once everyone had calmed down.

"Yes, but I want it to be a surprise," she hedged.

"Not a problem, just give me a call and we'll set up a time."

"This is going to be great so exciting," Nan said, clapping her hands and bouncing in her seat a little.

"You'll be in good hands, Nan," Kellen said, "Alex is a great artist." Alex looked down at her plate uncomfortably at Kellen's praise, and the move didn't go unnoticed by Javi. He gave the pair a sour look, but continued to eat his food. I made a mental note to talk to Alex about that as soon as everyone was gone.

Once everyone had pushed away from the table to either unbutton their pants or go change completely, I started clearing the table. I figured I'd give people an hour or so to digest before I brought out dessert.

"Hey, give me that," Reid said, coming up from behind me as I picked up a platter of mashed potatoes.

"Why?" I asked, confused. He couldn't seriously still be hungry; he'd eaten two full platefuls and a third helping of turkey. I was surprised he wasn't already passed out in a tryptophan coma.

"You cooked, we'll clean. You girls go sit down and relax, we'll do the dishes," Reid insisted, despite the grumbling from my brother and the outright bitching from Knox, which of course got him a healthy smack from Nan.

"Shit, you don't have to tell me twice," I said and led the other girls into the living room.

Twenty-Seven

Presents and Pack Mules

"Did you take a shit?" I asked Knox.

"Did you just ask me if I took a shit? What the fuck is wrong with you?"

"Yes, I did. Every time we go to the store, you get sudden onset diarrhea and you have to go to the bathroom, then you're gone for like an hour. This is game day, dude. This is Black Friday shopping. I need you to be present and focused, okay? No disappearing or diarrhea bullshit. So, shit now or forever hold your sphincter."

"Be honest, how good are these deals? Is it really worth staying up all fucking night to shop at four in the morning?"

"Yes, it's the only way I'm going to be able to buy presents for everybody this year."

"And why do you need me there again?" Knox asked. He was sprawled out on the couch, one hand strategically placed in the waistband of his jeans and the other holding the remote, altogether looking like a 2015 version of Al Bundy.

"To carry shit and ward off the fucking crazy ass shoppers that are gonna bite my fucking finger off trying to get a Teletubby."

"Why would you need a Teletubby?"

"It's a figure of speech, dickhead."

"I'm pretty sure it's not, twat face."

"It doesn't matter. I'm at an age where it's socially unacceptable for me to give people homemade cookies and call it a day. I'm supposed to be like a real fucking adult now."

"Could have fooled me, you've got fuzzy dice hanging from your rearview mirror."

"Yes but I also have the matching fuzzy handcuffs hanging from my headboard. See, adult, right here." I said pointing my thumbs at my chest.

It was midnight on Thanksgiving. I'd told Reid that he wasn't allowed to go shopping with us and interestingly enough he didn't put up a fight. I had no idea what I was going to get him for Christmas but if I found it tonight, I was not going to risk him being there to see me buy it.

Alex and I were all about the Black Friday shopping. Evie reluctantly went with us every year, but this time we were bringing in the big guns. At least that's how Knox referred to himself and my brother. Evie wanted to get the new 3D T.V. for her dad and we needed the brute force of tweedle dee and tweedle dum to wade through the crowds of psycho shoppers to get it. Not to mention the pair of them were like fucking pack mules. We could load them up and they'd just keep truckin' along, no need for the hassle of a bulky cart.

***

"This is bullshit," Knox grumbled.

"Quit your bitching," Kellen said, punching him in the arm. It was a good thing my brother spoke up because if I had to listen to Knox's whinny ass for another two hours I was going to castrate him. We'd been standing in line for over an hour waiting for Target to open. Alex and I had combed through the ads after dinner and made our plan of attack. We'd condensed all of our shopping to just three stores today, which was pretty minimal considering last year we shopped from four in the morning, all the way into the afternoon, breaking our long-standing record by hitting up eleven stores. We'd been exhausted and our legs were like Jell-O but we'd brought in an impressive haul.

There aren't many things I wouldn't do for a good sale. I mean, it's like girl code to never pay full price. Have you ever noticed the phenomena when a woman is complemented on an article of clothing or a purse and she automatically responds with where she got it and how much she paid for it? Like, 'Hey Claire, nice top!' 'Oh, thanks! I got it at Old Navy for only $4.95!' the 'Ha, bitch' is silent. It's as if the compulsion to prove our thriftiness is ingrained in our DNA. It's almost involuntary, like one of Pavlov's dogs, it's an instinctive response. If you didn't notice it before, you will now.

This year was all mapped out; we'd break into teams; Alex and Kellen would go for the electronics. The department on black Friday was like a motherfucking war zone, we needed our most intimidating and aggressive people there. If things got dicey Kellen could extract Alex before security was called. We didn't need another incident like 2012 on our hands. Thank God they hadn't pressed charges; we'd just been banned from that particular Walmart for a year. I would go for movies and cookware with Knox since I needed to keep an eye on the little cocksucker to make sure his head was in the game. Evie would head straight for the checkout line and hold our place. If everything went as planned, we should be in and out in less than an hour.

***

"Jesus, this is a lot of shit," Evie said as we looked around at the haul we'd lugged into the living room. Kellen and Knox had fled as soon as the plethora of shit we'd bought was unloaded. It was just as well; their services were no longer needed.

"I'll make some coffee," Alex called out as she headed for the kitchen.

"What? Why?" Evie asked in a weak and confused voice.

"We have to sort everything out and wrap it," I responded patiently. Evie hadn't gone through the whole Black Friday experience with us before, if we could convince her in the past to come shopping she'd peace out before the wrapping commenced.

"But, it's six in the morning," she whined.

"It's fine, you can go to bed if you want," Alex said coming back into the room. "Besides, you suck at wrapping."

"She's right!" Evie exclaimed, "I'm terrible at wrapping gifts, my dad and I used to wrap presents in the comic section of the newspaper, I don't have the pretty wrapping gene."

I laughed, "It's fine, go crash. We'll wrap the stuff you got for your dad."

"Have I told you lately how much I love you?" she asked as she slowly backed out of the living room and into the hallway before spinning around and rushing to her bedroom as if we could change our minds at any moment.

Alex handed me a mug of coffee before settling on the floor on the opposite end of the pile. We'd developed a system after so many years, we'd pull everything out and remove the price tags and sort them by receiver, cross checking to make sure we'd gotten everything we needed to cover everyone on our list. Then, and only then, we'd commence wrapping. Once we got started there'd be bows, ribbon and tags everywhere so we had to be organized going in, otherwise it would be

Christmas chaos.

"So," I started after we'd been at it for a half hour. "What was up with you and Kellen at dinner?"

"What do you mean?" Alex asked, sounding suspiciously cool.

"You got weird when he complimented your work, almost like you were embarrassed. What was that all about?"

"It was nothing. I guess I was just being modest."

"Pfft, since when?"

"Ugh, fine. He came in the other day to get a tattoo and things got a little weird. It's no big deal, I just got a little flustered."

"He didn't tell me he was getting a new tattoo, why was it weird? You've tattooed him plenty of times before." I said, wondering what my idiot brother did to make her uncomfortable.

"It's not, we were just being awkward around each other for no reason. We figured it out, no worries."

"But—"

"Drop it, Briar," she said, cutting me off.

"Okaaay," I relented. There was definitely more to the story but pushing Alex when she'd been up for over 24 hours was not my idea for a good time. Eventually I'd get it out of her.

An hour later, everything was wrapped and piled neatly under the tree. Alex and I stood back admiring our handiwork.

"I'm all done, I already got your gift hidden away. What about you?" Alex asked, knowing full well there was only one glaring unchecked name on my list. Reid.

"I have no idea what to get him, there's nothing he wants. Hell, we haven't even discussed if we're exchanging gifts or not," I complained.

"You are," Alex said quickly.

My head snapped in her direction, my eyes immediately narrowed on her face. "Do you know something I don't?" I asked accusingly, looking for any sign that she knew more than she'd let on before.

"No," Alex said rolling her eyes, "but come on. You guys have gotten pretty serious these past few months, it's safe to say you'll be exchanging Christmas presents."

"What am I supposed to get him? I've never had a boyfriend this time of year, what if I get him some cheesy gift and then he gets me something extravagant? Or the other way around, that would be even worse!"

"Calm your tits, woman. Reid isn't the extravagant type, at least not in the way of cost. Get him something that's meaningful, it doesn't matter how much you spend, with this guy it really is the thought that counts."

"But that's the problem, I have no thoughts!" I argued.

"Oh man, so many jokes," Alex said shaking her head. "Why don't you talk to Emma, see if she has any ideas?"

"That's a good one, she's known him for a while, and she sees him all the time. If anything, she can fish for information for me."

"See, you've got a plan. Now please go to bed, you're about two seconds away from a padded room."

"Good idea, night," I said and headed towards the oasis that was my bed.

Twenty-Eight

Who Wants a Snowgarita?

"Don't you have a T.V. at your place?" I asked as my douche of a brother plopped his ass down on my couch. Kellen and Knox had blown into the house and commandeered my living room without a single please or thank you.

Bastards.

"Yeah, but I wanted to spend time with my sister. Besides, I bought you this thing last year for Christmas," he said pointing to the giant T.V. mounted on the wall. "I can come over and watch it any time I want."

"Hmm, I don't think that's how it's supposed to work. In fact, I'm not exactly sure why you even bought me this monstrosity. Although, it did come in handy when the girls and I watched Magic Mike in all his glory on 65 inches of drool worthy HD. So, you want to explain why you need

277

to come here to watch the game when you have the exact same T.V. at your house? You know it's supposed to snow, right?"

"First, they always say it's going to snow, and we end up getting a half an inch of snow that turns into slush by midafternoon. Second, we're here because you have better food."

"Yeah," Knox called out. "Make us some sandwiches, woman."

Thankfully my brother punched him in the shoulder before I had a chance to react, otherwise, there was a good chance I would have pulled a Lorena Bobbitt on his ass.

I left the boys and Evie, who they adopted as an honorary dude whenever sports were on, to their own devices and headed for the kitchen. I had already planned to make a big dinner, so one more mouth to feed wasn't a big deal. Yes, one, because I'd be damned if Knox was getting anything other than ramen for dinner after his little comment. Hopefully it'd teach the little shitlord to think before insulting the woman he expected to feed him.

***

"Wow, it's really starting to come down out there," Alex said, from her perch on the window bench. "I doubt I'll open the studio tomorrow if it keeps up like this."

"No shit? It's actually sticking?" I asked,

rushing over to pull the curtain back more fully. There were several inches of fluffy white powder covering the driveway and untouched street in front of the house. "I hope it keeps up, I could use a snow day."

"Pfft," Reid scoffed, coming up behind me to look out the window. "This is nothing, when I was growing up we didn't get a snow day unless the plows couldn't get through, and that almost never happened."

"Well it's different here, we have hills to worry about. A little snow can really fuck shit up." I argued.

"I lived on a mountain," Reid deadpanned.

"Whatever."

"Hmm, I love it when you say that," Reid said slipping his hands around my waist.

I turned my head and glared at him. Because goddamn it, I hated the fact that he got off on making me flustered.

Just then, the local news jingle came blasting through the speakers, interrupting the football game everyone had been watching.

"We interrupt your regularly scheduled broadcast to bring you breaking news. A severe weather alert has been issued for the following counties..." I tuned out the news to focus on Knox throwing a full blown hissy fit.

"This is bullshit!" he said, throwing one of our decorative pillows across the room.

"Hey, fucker! That shit was expensive," I

yelled.

"Dude, Wilson was about to run the ball!"

"*Dude*," I mocked. "No one gives a fuck, it's snowing!" I said, pointing to the T.V. where sure enough the words 'Snowacalypse 2015' were displayed boldly above the list of school closures scrolling across the bottom of the screen.

"If schools are closed, I wonder if the clinic is going to close," Evie said as she typed out a message on her phone.

"Knox and I aren't on shift tomorrow," Kellen said, popping open another beer. "So it doesn't matter much to us."

Just then, my phone vibrated in my pocket. I pulled it out to read a mass text message from the business continuity team declaring that the office would indeed be closed the next day. "Score! We're closed tomorrow!"

"Us too," Evie called out.

"What about you?" I asked Reid, turning in his arms.

Reid laughed, "We brew 24/7 babe, there are people at the warehouse now. I'll probably keep the bar closed though, I doubt anyone is going to come in for a drink anyways."

"But will *you* have to go in?"

"Yes, fermentation stops for no man."

"That sucks," I complained.

"If it makes you feel better I'll hate every minute of it," he said pulling me closer. I wrapped my arms around him and snuggled into his chest.

"Liar. You love your job."

"I do, but I—" Reid started to reply but was interrupted by Alex making a gaging noise.

"Gross. Enough with the lovey dovey shit, you guys are going to make me puke," she said, getting up from her spot by the window. "I've got to go re-schedule appointments. I'll be back out in a bit."

That was weird.

I watched Alex's retreating back as she headed to her bedroom. Something was going on with her but she wouldn't tell me or Evie what it was. It killed me she didn't want to talk to me about whatever was bothering her. Alex wasn't much of a sharer, at least not when it came to anything having to do with emotions. I just had to trust that she'd eventually clue me in.

"Okaaay," I said. "Who wants margaritas?"

Evie looked up from her phone. "Shit, I think we're almost out of tequila," she said.

"Sweetheart, have you learned nothing from our years of friendship? We may run out of vodka or rum, occasionally we might run out of whiskey, but we will never run out of tequila," I said as I made my way into the kitchen. I grabbed the stepstool I kept in the kitchen for just such an occasion and walked over to the fridge. Climbing up, I opened the cabinet above and started blindly fumbling around until my fingertips touched cool glass. I pulled out the giant bottle of 1800 and presented it to Evie. "See, there is always a spare."

"I should have never doubted you," she laughed.

* * *

"Dude, I'm not made of money."

"Since when is having an ice maker constitute as being made of money?" Knox argued.

"It's a luxury item, like two ply toilet paper," I slurred. We were two pitchers of margaritas and half a game of Cards Against Humanity into our snowed in party and I'd just discovered that we were out of ice.

"Wait, I got it." Reid said. He opened the sliding glass door and walked out onto the deck. Coming back with a bowl full of ice and snow he packed a cup and added the tequila and mixer.

"See babe, it's a snowgarita!" Reid exclaimed, beaming at me. His goofy smile causing those lines around his eyes to appear.

I laughed loudly. "Oh my God! I love you!"

As soon as the words left my lips I wanted to snatch them back. Reid didn't say anything in response or look surprised at my confession. His grin just grew and those lines got deeper. I wanted the floor to open up and suck me down into the fiery depths of Hell. Being the devil's personal bitch would've had nothing on the embarrassment I was feeling.

Not knowing what to do or say, I turned to the group holding the cup up, "Snowgarita, anyone?"

We got back to our game, and if it was possible it got even more depraved than before. You don't really know someone until you play Cards Against Humanity with them. By eleven, everyone was hammered and we were losing people at a rapid pace. Evie had crawled, yes crawled, to her room, mumbling about how tequila shots between margaritas had been a bad idea. Knox was sawing logs in the living room, his giant body taking up the entire couch.

"Let's go to bed, I want sex," I slurred to Reid.

He laughed, "Okay, sounds good to me." He hadn't had as much to drink as I had but he was still pretty toasted in his own right. We got up from the table to go to the bedroom, at least we tried. It was more like we ping-ponged down the hallway, bouncing from one wall to the other. Alcohol may have been a factor in our increased silliness, but the uncontrollable laughter was the reason for our inability to walk in a straight line. At one point, we even tried to do the *Wizard of Oz* yellow brick road walk and ended up in a heap on the floor.

Once we made it to my room and had managed to get naked, we collapsed on the bed. I started to realize that drunk sex when you still had a stomach full of liquid sloshing around might not have been my brightest idea.

Fuck it.

Reid started kissing my neck, his hand sliding down my stomach and in between my legs to tease me. It felt good, it felt even better when he moved down the bed and replaced is fingers with his tongue. Twenty minutes later, it still felt good, but I was beginning to realize that I was not going to make it to the finish line tonight. Nope, I had the dreaded whiskey clit. No matter what, I was not getting off until I sobered up.

I thought about stopping him. It would have been the decent thing to do, but I was holding out hope that I might be wrong about my alcohol induced affliction. Convincing myself that I'd give it five more minutes and if nothing by then, I'd let him come up for air.

"Briar, hey!" Reid whisper-shouted. "Did you fall asleep?"

"Wha-what, no! Of course, not!" I said groggily, rubbing my eyes.

I did, I totally did. In fact, there might have been some drool on my face. Jesus, how long had I been out?

"I can't believe you fell asleep while I was going down on you! Honestly, I don't know how to feel about that."

I cringed, "I'm sorry, I'm just really drunk."

Reid busted out laughing, which in turn caused me to fall into a fit of giggles. I tried to catch my breath, but I couldn't. It was just too funny.

"I can't believe you fell asleep," Reid wheezed.

"I'm sorry!" I said when I finally stopped laughing. "Can we go to bed now? The room is starting to spin."

"Yeah, you better sleep it off, because you're going to have to make that up to me later."

"Scouts honor, I'll give you the best blowjob of your life as soon as I'm sober again."

"Blowjob? It's going to take more than that to make up for falling asleep on me, I'm thinking anal."

"Oh my God! I thought you were a good person. I can't believe you're trying to guilt me into anal while I'm drunk."

"I'm a man, I had to try," he said, pulling me closer so my back was to his front. He threw the blanket over both of us and I settled into him, quickly succumbing to sleep.

Twenty-Nine

From Zero to Bitch Mode

Coffee. I needed coffee. I was like a druggie searching for their next fix as I shuffled through the office Wednesday morning in search of caffeine. It was only nine in the morning and I was already having a shit-tastic day.

It all started when I noticed we were out of coffee at the house, how that was possible with a certifiably insane coffee addict like Alex in the house I didn't know. Then, I slipped and fell on my ass in the driveway on the way to my car, soaking my pants and forcing me to go back into the house and change. My impromptu wardrobe change set me back ten minutes, which wouldn't have been a big deal if everyone and their mother didn't forget how to fucking drive when there was slush on the road. My 20-minute commute turned into nearly an hour of screaming at every driver within a six-block radius.

When I finally got to work, I discovered that they had failed to plow, shovel, or salt the parking lot. This created an icy, slushy, moat at the entrance, which of course, my car got stuck in. After I called Mr. Piddle Pants (Kyle from marketing) to pull me out, I made my way into the office a damp and frazzled mess.

Just as I was bringing my mug to my lips, ready to enjoy just a moment of peace and hopefully turn my day around, Queen Bitch walked into the break room.

"Good morning, Briar," Nova chirped in her stupid musical Disney princess voice.

Fucking cunt.

"Morning," I responded, finally taking a sip of my coffee, which of course burned the shit out of my tongue.

Why me? Seriously, what the fuck did I do to deserve karma fucking me in the ass without lube today?

"Did you enjoy your snow day? I can't believe they shut down the office like that for less than a foot of snow. A few snow flurries and the whole town shuts down, back home it's just another day. But you'll see that soon enough, Bend is amazing in the winter, you'll love it!" she said excitedly.

It took a minute for my brain to catch up with her words. I was, after all operating at less than full capacity.

"I'm sorry, what?" I asked numbly.

"Christmas, silly. Reid's parents throw this huge party every year on Christmas eve. They go all out; their house is like a winter wonderland. You've been to their house, right?"

"Uh, no I haven't."

"Oh, well I'm sure you just haven't gotten over there yet, but you'll be at the party, right? Everyone comes, it's *the* can't miss event of the year."

Did we just get teleported into an episode of The OC*? Reid said his parents were rich and had rich friends but it was just a party, right?*

"I don't know we haven't really talked about it," I said.

"Oh sorry didn't mean to let the cat out the bag or anything. I just assumed," she said innocently.

"It's fine, we just haven't talked about Christmas yet."

"Of course. Well then, I'll just get back to work," she said, giving me a look of pity and strutting out the door.

I went through my whole day in a fog. Why hadn't Reid asked me to go with him to his family's party? Was he planning on going? Except for the one time, he never talked about his family in any sort of depth. It irked me to no end that Nova knew him and his family better than I did. I mean I was his girlfriend, right?

At dinner that night I struggled trying to find

a way to broach the subject. It wasn't a big deal, he probably just forgot to mention it. My insecurities were getting the best of me as I tried to rationalize why Reid hadn't mentioned anything about Christmas. It was two weeks away; I probably should have brought it up earlier but since he'd spent Thanksgiving with us I'd just assumed that he would spend Christmas with us too.

Stop letting that bitch get in your head and just ask him.

"So umm," I started, causing Reid to look up from his sandwich.

"What's up?"

"Nova said something interesting at work today…" I trailed off, feeling incredibly uncomfortable bringing it up.

"Okay? Babe, what's the matter?" Reid asked, as he set down his food to give me his full attention, and a worried look creased his brow.

Taking a deep breath, I just let it spill out, "She said something about your family's Christmas eve party?"

The worried look instantly cleared from his face. "Oh yeah, things have been busy and I completely forgot," he said.

Relief rushed through me, it had just slipped his mind. No conspiracy, he just forgot to mention it, thank fuck.

"It's this totally pretentious thing that my parents do every year with all their friends from the club. Don't worry, I would never put you through that."

Boyfriend needing a lobotomy say what?

"So, you don't want me to meet your family?" I asked.

"No, they're assholes, and their friends are just as bad. Trust me you are way better off staying home."

Well, this isn't how I thought this conversation was going to go.

"But you're going?" I asked.

"Unfortunately," he sighed. "I have to go; my grandfather is going to be there. I need to give him the last payment from the loan he gave me when I started the brewery. Sure, I could pop it in the mail but getting to see the look on my father's face when I hand it over is going to be priceless."

Reid was grinning at me, like I was in on the joke, but I wasn't. All I'd heard was 'no I don't want you to meet my family'.

"Besides, my grandfather is getting up there in age, it'd be nice to spend some time with him. Don't worry, I'll be back Christmas day and we can do our thing then."

Up until this point I'd assumed Reid was a smart man, obviously, I'd been wrong.

"But Nova's going, you guys are going to be there together, with your family." I confirmed.

"Well yeah, I mean she'll be there with her family. Our parents are friends and they do business together, she always goes," he shrugged.

I couldn't believe he didn't see where I was

290

going with my line of questioning. His ex-girlfriend being at a family party without his current girlfriend was kind of a problem for me. I mean if we were as serious as he made it seem like we were, then I should meet his family eventually.

"Look, don't get in your head about it," Reid said gently, reaching out to give my hand a light squeeze. "It's a stupid party and if I didn't have to go, I wouldn't. But I have to be there and I don't want to put you through that."

"So you never want me to meet your family?" I asked. I wasn't trying to be the crazy girlfriend but I couldn't shake the feeling that maybe I was taking this relationship more seriously than Reid was.

"No, no, no, it's not like that. It's just if you meet my family I want you to meet them one-on-one not in a huge cocktail party setting. They're less likely to be assholes if you're with them without an audience. Otherwise, they'll eat you alive. I'm so sorry, I don't want you to feel bad about this it's just not the right time."

All right nothing to freak out about, Evie was always telling me to stop overthinking things and just let it go, so what did it matter that he met my parents and I haven't met his yet? It didn't mean anything. Reid was awesome, he was sweet and thoughtful. If he really didn't think that it was a good idea for me to meet his parents yet, then I would just have to trust his judgment. I was just going to let it ride.

I'd done a good job of letting the whole Christmas party thing go. It still stung that I wasn't going but I trusted Reid and for now, that had to be enough.

It was the day before Reid left for Bend and I was wrapping up some work before the start of the long weekend. I was just about to pack up my things and head out when Nova popped her head into my office. I'd ignored her for the better part of the last two weeks but if the smile on her face was any indication, she hadn't noticed.

"Hey, Briar, there's something wrong with my phone and I can't get a hold of Reid. Can you let him know I'll be ready to go around 10 tomorrow? He has the address."

"What?" I asked, a sense of dread brewing in my stomach.

"He's picking me up tomorrow and we're driving to Bend together. My car won't make it over the pass with as much snow as we've been getting. Didn't he tell you?" her tone was innocent but the barely-there smirk that teased the corners of her mouth told me she knew he hadn't.

I'd been suspicious of her since the beginning, but she'd given me no reason to think that she wanted anything to do with Reid other than friendship, that was until the little things started to add up. The way she reacted to seeing him stop by the office when I'd first started, the picture on her desk, casually mentioning the Christmas party, and now this.

"Must have slipped his mind, I'll let him know."

"Thanks," she said with not an ounce of appreciation in her voice. Instead of leaving she walked further into my office and stood over my desk. "I'm so happy we have this opportunity to ride over together, it will be great to catch up, you know reminisce about old times."

She gave me a little smirk. Yeah, 'reminisce' I knew exactly what that meant. She just went from zero to bitch mode in three seconds flat. It was like all of a sudden the veil was lifted and her conniving little ass was revealed.

"I'm sure, I'll let him know. If you don't mind I have a few things to finish up," I said, keeping my voice steady. I wouldn't give her the satisfaction of a reaction, at least not now.

"Of course, if I don't see you before you leave, have a good holiday," she said as she glided out of my office. No joke the bitch glided, must be some demonic gift the dark lord gave her because there was no way she was anything short of the spawn of Satan.

Snatching my phone off my desk, I called Reid. I couldn't believe he'd let me walk into her trap a second time. The phone rang three times and I was about to hang up and text him when he answered.

"Hey babe."

"Hey, interesting thing just happened. Nova came in and told me to let you know she was going to be ready for you to pick her up at ten tomorrow. Is there something you forgot to tell me?" I kept my voice even, no use in getting mad at him right out of the gate.

"Oh, shit. Yeah, she called me last night and asked for a ride. Her car won't make it over the pass"

Right, never mind the fact that she went home for Thanksgiving and her car seemed to do just fucking fine.

"Don't you think it's kind of odd?"

"What?" he asked, sounding thoroughly confused.

"She suddenly can't drive herself, I can't believe you don't see what she's doing," I said getting progressively louder.

"Briar, trust me, Nova is just a friend."

"Maybe to you, but she wants you back, it's obvious," I sighed heavily. "Look, I know I sound crazy, but she wants you back. She specifically came into my office to rub it in my face and tell me how good it will be to have alone time with you to *reminisce*." The contempt in my voice was clear.

"What did she say exactly?"

"It's not what she said, it's how she said it."

"I'm sorry it makes you uncomfortable, but I already told her I would give her a ride. I'll talk to her tomorrow and make sure everything is copasetic. I'm sure it's just a misunderstanding. Really, she was engaged to Brad for a long time, if anything she's hung up on him, not me."

Realizing I wasn't going to get anywhere with Reid on this until I had some hard proof, I decided to drop it.

"Okay."

"We still on for dinner tonight?" Reid asked, sounding a little unsure.

"Of course, I just have one more thing I have to do at the office and then I'll meet you at your place?"

"Sounds good, see you in a bit."

"Bye," I said, disconnecting the call. Reid clearly didn't understand how women worked, I was going to have to set this cum guzzling demon slut straight. I'd be damned if I was going to let her be the Angelina to my Jennifer.

I grabbed my purse and headed out, but instead of leaving the building I marched right into Nova's office.

"Briar," she said sweetly. "To what do I owe the pleasure?"

"Cut the crap, bitch." I said. Instantly her façade fell away.

"Excuse you?" she asked. "You come into *my* office and call me a b—"

"I want to make one thing abundantly clear," I said interrupting her.

"By all means," she said waiving her hand for me to proceed.

"Reid is mine. You need to back the hell off; do you understand me?"

"Oh sweetheart," she said her voice dripping with condescension. "Reid and I share a history, something you don't have. It's been written in the cards since we were in diapers, you don't stand a chance."

I laughed without humor, "That's where you're wrong," I said, placing my hands on my hips. "We're not gonna be playing this game anymore, Nova. I know exactly who you are and what's more Reid knows exactly who you are and what you're trying to pull."

I saw fear flash through her eyes before they turned to ice, "I got you hired here and I can get you fired," she said.

"So do it," I dared. "It's not going to get Reid to take you back."

"We'll see about that. Reid may be having fun with you for now, but that will all change over Christmas. I'm telling you right now, his parents have more pull than you think."

"You know what, I don't even know why I'm in here. It's not like I have anything to worry about. Reid doesn't want you, and no matter what you're planning it's not gonna work. It's pathetic, trying to recreate the past after your fiancé kicked you to the curb. Next time you might want to keep the real you tucked away until *after* the wedding."

Nova was far less striking when she was mad, her face was red and blotchy and her nostrils flared as she breathed heavily. If I didn't know any better, I'd think she was about to launch herself over her desk and tackle me. I gave her a pitying look for good measure before turning on my heel and marching out of the office.

Thirty

Assholes and Apologies

I thought he was my person. The one that made my chest ache every time I looked at him. The one that could make my heart race with just one smile. The one that could take my breath away with a single chuckle. The one that made every day brighter.

I was curled up on the floor under the Christmas tree, clutching a bottle of wine and staring at the picture on my phone that made my heart feel like it was cracking in two. I'd gotten the text exactly twenty-seven minutes ago, and I was already well on my way to a drunken stupor.

It was a picture of Reid and Nova, his arm around her shoulder and his head tipped back in laughter at something she'd said. The whore had her head on his shoulder, one arm wrapped around his middle and the other hand resting flat on his chest. The text message had come from Nova with the caption *He was never yours.*

In a moment of anger, I forwarded the text to Reid with my own caption: *is this why you didn't want me to come?* He had replied a few times since, but I didn't respond to any of them. I hadn't even opened them to read what he had to say.

The picture may have seemed innocent to unsuspecting eyes, but the intimacy of the way she was touching him and the easy way he held her spoke volumes to me. It didn't matter how long you'd known someone. You don't cuddle your ex at a family party that your current girlfriend wasn't invited to. At least you didn't if the ex was still an ex.

I just stared at the picture and cried.

Sitting all by myself on Christmas Eve drinking a bottle of wine under the tree, I didn't think I'd ever felt more alone in my life. Alex and Evie had gone to bed before the text came in so they had no idea what was going on. I supposed it was for the best, I didn't feel like talking about how my heart was bleeding out all over the place.

However, being left alone to my own thoughts and inner reflection just allowed my mind to wander down the rabbit hole. It had all happened exactly how I'd feared. The falling was scary but fun, exciting even, but the landing hurt like hell. My whole body ached and my eyes burned with hot tears as they slipped down my face.

The evil wench had won. He was with his family. The same family he hadn't wanted to introduce me to. The girls had tried to talk me down, tried to tell me that it wasn't that big of a deal. He was just going home to see his family and eventually he'd introduce me. But to me, it was Reid telling me that I didn't mean enough to him to be permitted to meet the people in his life. Not Nova though, she was there, she belonged there.

So here I sat, wallowing in pain and self-pity. I couldn't understand how Evie could go through this over and over again and come back still wanting more. I was crushed, I never wanted to feel pain like this again.

It had felt like he was ripping away the piece of my heart I'd given him as soon as he drove away. Because even though he'd said he'd be back in a few days, I knew deep down it was the beginning of the end. I wouldn't compete for him, I shouldn't have to, not if he was really mine. I wanted to be important enough for him to choose me, but I guess I wasn't.

I tried to turn off my brain, it hurt too much to think about. I could live without him, I knew that. I could go on with my life and find happiness somewhere, but I didn't want to. That revelation caused me to curl even further into myself. Abandoning the bottle of wine, I wrapped my arms around my knees. Squeezing myself tight in an effort to keep the broken pieces of my heart from spilling out on the floor. My sniffles turned into silent sobs as I let myself feel the ache of losing the person I loved.

A loud pounding on the front door woke me from my restless sleep. I quietly tiptoed around the couch and towards the entry, making sure to grab the bat we kept propped up on the side table, just in case. You couldn't be too careful. I'd seen all those horror movies with the creepy guy knocking on the unsuspecting girl's door in the middle of the night asking to use the telephone.

Fuck that.

I briefly considered waking up Alex and Evie for back up but decided against it. I didn't even know what time it was. Looking through the peep hole I gasped in shock when I saw Reid.

What the fuck?

I swung open the door to find a wet and shivering Reid on my porch.

"Wha—" I began but he cut me off.

"When you wouldn't return my texts or calls I jumped in my car and drove all night. Briar, please you have to listen to me. It wasn't what it looked like, I swear!" His voice was desperate and choppy, his eyes imploring me to give him a chance.

I was uneasy and still upset but I couldn't leave him out in the rain like that. Pulling open the door more fully I waved him inside. I'd listen to what he had to say, but I doubted it would change my mind. If you couldn't trust the one you were with, you'd never be happy.

Once I shut the door behind him, he launched into his explanation. "It wasn't what it looked like, I swear to God, Briar. I would never—" Reid's voice broke, and he had to take a second to clear his throat before he was able to continue. "My mom was trying to get a group picture, she told me to put my arm around Nova so I did. I didn't even think about it. Then Lana said something and I laughed, that must have been when Sasha took the picture. I thought it was weird the way Nova was acting so I moved away from her. I didn't realize what was going on until I got that text from you."

"Who's Sasha? And how do you know she was the one that took the picture?" I asked, it seemed a little too convenient that he had the entire story put together.

"She's Nova's mom. When I saw the picture, I lost it. I made a huge scene, screaming at Nova in front of everyone. Her mom jumped in and started spouting off a bunch of bullshit, that's when I put two and two together. My mom might have been in on it too. Fuck, I don't know. This is so messed up. This is why I didn't want you to have to deal with them, they're all fucking crazy, who does that shit?"

"I warned you about Nova and you brushed me off."

"Briar. Babe, please. Hand to my heart, I honestly didn't think Nova was like that. When we were kids we would complain about how horrible our parents were and how we'd never be like them. You have to understand; we were friends our entire life before we ever got involved. I thought I could trust her."

"That's the problem, you trusted her. Not me."

Reid stepped closer to me, taking my head in his hands and forcing me to look at him. I was shocked to see tears in his eyes when he spoke, "I am so sorry. Please, believe me. I can't lose you. I was going crazy on the drive over here, I had four hours to think of all they ways this could play out. I don't blame you for being mad, I deserve it. But don't let this be the end. I'm begging you, please forgive me."

I wanted to give in, my heart was aching to tell him I forgave him and let him hold me the way he always did. But my brain was at war with my heart, telling me that it was too easy. It shouldn't be that simple of a fix, not after what I'd gone through that night. When I didn't say anything, Reid continued to argue his case.

"I was an idiot, Briar. I wanted to show my dad that I'd made my own way, I was so focused on proving him wrong that I turned into a total asshole. I didn't think about how that could hurt you, I'm so sorry. I'm not that guy, you know I'm not that guy. I just got lost for a while. Even before all that shit with Nova went down, I was miserable because you weren't with me. I couldn't focus on anything anyone said, all I could think about was you being here and me being there and how wrong it felt. Because I always want to be where you are, no matter what you're doing I just want to be near you all the time. You could be painting a fucking wall and I'd want to be in the same room with you because you're the most fascinating person I've ever met. You're the brightest part of every day. Briar, I love you."

My heart squeezed in my chest and tears spilled from my eyes. I'd been waiting to hear those words for months, and he's going to pull them out now? In the middle of our first real fight?

"You love me? You're going to drop that on me right now? You think that's just going to fix everything?" I asked.

"I said it because it's true. Because whenever something good happens to me you're the first person I want to tell. Because I miss you every moment of every day that I'm not with you. Because you crawled under my skin the first time we fought over white chocolate versus milk chocolate and I never want to stop having that fight, ever."

"But why now?" I asked. I wanted to believe him, I wanted to forgive him. But I couldn't help but wonder if it was just a reaction to the fear of losing me.

"Because you're finally ready to hear it. Let me show you something," he said. Walking around the couch, he rummaged underneath the

Christmas tree, moving around boxes in search of something.

"What are you doing?" I asked.

"I put something here before I left and I think you're finally ready to see it," he stood up with a gift bag and a card in hand. "Merry Christmas, open the card first." He said handing me the gift.

I walked over to the couch and sat down, Reid following closely behind me. As soon as I opened the card a small piece of paper floated out. Picking it up with shaky hands, I turned it over. "Oh my God," I whispered, my eyes bouncing between Reid and the sketch. It was a rough sketch of me, or my face to be more exact. My eyes were closed and my hair was wild on the pillow. It was beautiful.

"Read the card," he prompted.

I took a deep breath and read the words scrawled on the inside of the card in his usual messy handwriting.

Briar,
This image is the first thing that I see on the backs of my eyelids when I wake up in the morning and the last thing I see when I go to bed at night. You're the most beautiful woman I've ever laid my eyes on. You make me laugh, you make me happy and you make me believe that anything is possible. I have loved you for four

*months, twenty-two days, twelve
hours and thirty-six minutes and I
would be honored if you'd let me love
you with all my heart and all my soul
for a million more.*
Love,
Reid

When I finished reading the card tears were
cascading down my face, coating my cheeks. I
looked up at Reid wanting to say something but not
able to form words. He just pushed the bag closer
to me, motioning for me to open it.

I opened the bag, pulling out a giant mason
jar filled with little scraps of folded green, blue, and
orange paper.

"The green ones are memories and
moments that we shared together, the blue ones
are reasons I love you, and the orange ones are my
dreams for our future."

"I love you so fucking much," I sobbed and
threw my arms around him. It wasn't eloquent or
romantic but it was honest.

"Look, I know it's quick and I know it's a lot
to take in. We can take our time, but can we do it
together? Because, I want to wake up with you
every morning, tell you that I love you, and then
spend the rest of the day proving it to you."

Thirty-One

Merry Christmas, Misfits

I loved him. I was *in* love with him. And he loved me back. A feeling of contentment blanketed me as we stayed cuddled on the couch for a long while, just letting it all sink in.

"The sun's coming up we should probably wake everyone up," I said, my voice muffled against Reid's chest.

"Why not just let them wake up on their own?"

"Because it's Christmas, I don't want to wait for their lazy asses. I want presents!" I disentangled myself from Reid's arms and stood up.

"Alright, I'll make coffee and then I'm going to jump in the shower," Reid said, getting to his feet.

"Good man," I said over my shoulder as I went off to wreak havoc.

Stomping down the hall I swung open the door to Alex's room and switched on the light. "Wake up bi—" I was cut off midsentence by a shriek and a thump as a body fell out of the bed. I cocked my head to the side at the scene before me.

Alex was still in bed, sitting up and clutching the covers to her chest. Her shoulders were bare and her hair was a ratted mess, the puzzle pieces started to click together.

"Who—" I began but was cut off by Alex's whispered shout.

"Close the door! I'll be out in a minute."

I smirked at her and stayed put, "You've got to be kidding me. You getting some Christmas lovin? Who's stuffing your stocking?" I asked teasingly.

"Get out!" she yelled at me and I watched in horror as my brother's head popped up on the other side of the bed.

"Whoa, what the fuck?" I shouted.

"Be quiet!" Alex hissed throwing pillow at my face. "Get the hell out of here!"

I backed out of the door laughing my ass off, finally he had stuck it to her. Go big brother! I walked across the hall to Evie's room. Since it had worked so well with Alex I decided to wake Evie in the same fashion. I burst through the door and flicked on the light.

"Rise and shine, bitch!"

"Fuuuuuuck yooooouuuuu!" she groaned and burrowed further into her cocoon of blankets.

She looked like a giant Evie burrito, just a little blonde bun popping out of the top. I walked into the room snatching a pillow and proceeded to beat her over the head with it.

"Come on, get up! I cannot be the only one up right now, it's against the laws of nature. We've got presents to open." Satisfied that I'd disturbed her enough that she wouldn't be able to go back to sleep I headed back to the kitchen where a pot of liquid gold was waiting for me.

Alex walked into the kitchen and I poured her a cup of coffee as well, heavy on the creamer, just how she liked it. I was going to need to butter her up if I was going to get any information out of her.

"So, how long have you been boinking my brother?" I teased.

"Shut up," she said taking the cup I held out for her.

"No, I'm curious. How long has this been going on and why didn't you tell me? Didn't you feel it the need to ask my permission before you slept with my brother?"

She knew I was teasing of course, but I had to give her shit. I mean she had to know that I would be giving her shit about this. Come to think of it, that's probably why she didn't tell me.

"Shut up Briar," she said in a monotone voice.

"Oh come on, Kellen and Alex sitting in a tree…" I began to sing.

"Shh!" she hissed at me as Evie walked into the room.

"Calm your tits Alex," Evie said shuffling past her, "I already knew."

"What? How?" she asked.

"Yeah, how did you know before me? He's my brother!" I questioned.

Ignoring me Evie addressed Alex directly, "You realize that we share a wall, right?"

"Shit," Alex winces, "sorry."

"Don't worry about it. I bought earplugs." Evie shrugged, leaning back on the counter sipping her freshly made coffee.

"But seriously Alex, were you going to tell me that you were seeing my brother?"

"We're not seeing each other," she said emphatically.

"So you're using him for sex? I don't know how I feel about that."

"We're using each other for sex, it's no big deal just leave it alone."

"Okay, fine," I said and gave Evie a curious look. She just shrugged and took another sip of her coffee. They were both adults, I needed to mind my own business, maybe. I'd talk to Kellen about it later and figure out what the hell was going on with the two of them.

"Reid, you're next. Here," I said, sliding his present out from behind the tree. It wasn't heavy but it was big and awkward. It took me a minute but I managed to drag it over to where he was sitting on the couch.

He tore into it excitedly. I was pretty sure by the shape he had an idea of what it was.

"Briar, I— this is amazing, how?" he asked, not taking his eyes off the canvas. I'd gotten together with Emma and had each of the kids at the youth center take the canvas and add something to it until it formed a sort of collage of their work. The canvas was a riot of color and different styles. It took a couple of weeks but they'd managed to finish it the previous week.

"Emma," I said simply.

"I can't believe you did this," he said as he set the painting down and pulled me to sit in his lap. "This is the best present I've ever gotten, thank you," he whispered in my ear.

I leaned back into his chest and watched my friends open the rest of their presents, providing commentary when necessary.

Once we were finished we cleaned up the mess of wrapping paper and I headed into the kitchen. There would be more presents to unwrap later, but for now I needed to get started cooking. Much like Thanksgiving, we'd planned to have the whole family over for brunch.

I'd even extended the olive branch and invited my father. It was a huge step for me, especially on Christmas since he'd soured the season for me for years. It wasn't an instant fix, I still had some pretty strong resentment toward him, but I was starting to realize that it wasn't my job to punish him for his actions. I was his daughter and I couldn't let one bad choice taint a lifetime of memories. I wasn't sure if we'd ever get back to the way we were, if it would ever be easy again, but I was willing to try.

As I moved about the kitchen cooking a meal for the most important people in my life, I realized how lucky I was to have a family who loved me, no matter how unconventional they were. The T.V. was on in the other room and people were laughing and some even shouting, but we were all together.

Abandoning the task at hand I snatched my cell off the counter and typed out a quick message and held my breath as I waited for an answer.

> **Me: What are your plans today?**
> **Emma: Nothing, Mom's working**
> **Me: Come over?**
> **Emma: Really? But it's Christmas, don't you have family coming over?**
> **Me: You are family, get your ass over here.**
> **Emma: OK ☺**

I quickly sent her the address and let out a heavy sigh. Just then, Reid came up behind me, pulling me back into his chest.

"Everything okay?" he asked.

"It is now," I said, because it was.

Emma turned up a half hour later. Reid

312

mouthed the words 'thank you' over her shoulder as he took her coat. I just shrugged, he didn't need to thank me for anything, Emma was one of us, this was where she belonged.

The meal was delicious and the table conversation colorful as always. It didn't take long for Emma to join in, laughing and joking with everyone like she'd always been there. I sat back and smiled to myself as I watched all my favorite people under one roof enjoying a meal together. No matter what happened in our lives, the people sitting around that table would be there for each other, unconditionally.

Sometimes the family you choose is the one you needed all along.

Epilogue

It was moving day again. Well, *technically* it was moving day. I'd been basically living with Reid for the last two months, but today we were making it official. Since Javi's lease was up on his apartment he'd agreed to move into the house, taking my room.

It was bittersweet. I loved living with my girls, but Reid and I paying for two different places when we spent every night together anyway wasn't very practical. Besides, it was time to move on and create a home with Reid. We weren't talking marriage or anything, at least not right at the moment. We'd had the conversation about what marriage and kids would look like for us, but that was still way off in the future. We were content with the way things were for now, we were happy.

Nova had been transferred back to the Bend office immediately following the episode at Reid's parents' Christmas party. Apparently, her parents wanted to prevent any further embarrassment on their part and figured removing her from the situation was the best option. Although, I would have liked to confront her about her little stunt, it wasn't necessary. It had all worked out.

"Hey, babe," Reid called to me as he came down the hall and into the living room. "I think this is it, will you go double check and make sure I didn't miss anything?"

"Sure."

As I walked down the hall I heard angry voices coming from Alex's room. The voices were low so I couldn't hear what was being said but they were definitely pissed. It sounded like Kellen. I wanted to eavesdrop but I resisted, moving further down the hall to my room.

Alex still hadn't told me what was going on with Kellen, but from what little information I was able to extract from my brother, they weren't seeing each other anymore. It took a lot of self-control not to push for more, but I'd managed. I was still holding out hope that they'd figure it out.

I glanced around my now barren room, taking in the empty space. Even though we'd only lived together for six months, it felt like the end of an era. I suppose it kind of was. Reid and I hadn't been together long, but I had no doubt in my mind that we'd eventually get married and start a family. It wasn't a matter of if, but when. The days of all of us being single and crazy together were in the past, and as happy as I was about finding Reid, I was a little bit nostalgic for the good old days.

Maybe I wasn't proud of everything in my past, but I didn't regret anything. Because without every misstep and wrong turn, I wouldn't have ended up where I was now. I would always look back and remember the good times, but I didn't actually want to go *back*. I was happy to move forward and start the next chapter.

I guess that was just a part of growing up.

Acknowledgements

Mom, thank you for bringing me up in a home full of laughter and shenanigans. No matter what the situation, you always found a way to find the funny. I get my humor from you so if this book isn't funny the readers now know who to blame.

Dani and Robo, my wonderful editors, I adore you. You put up with my comma loving, period allergic ass and for that, I am eternally grateful. You guys are amazing, thank you for sticking with me and your kind words.

Cassy, you are a Queen! I believe my words when I saw this cover were 'Holy Fuck' and I have the same reaction every time I look at it. You are an amazing designer and professional. There will never be another, you're stuck with me! Thank you for the work you put into this cover and I can't wait to work with you again!

To my girls, you guys inspire me every day. For years, I've been saying 'that's going to go in a book one day'. Well, guess what? Today's the day. I love you all.

About The Author

K.A Ware is an indie author living in Ridgefield, Washington with her husband and daughter. Her days consist of surfing the internet while pretending to write, making soap, and avoiding eye contact with an ever growing pile of laundry.

Writing is not her only passion, K.A. also serves on the Board of Directors for a local non-profit and spends way too much time reading. She believes in the power of words, alpha females, and that special escape you get when you hunker down and dig into a good book.

When she's not busy mothering, working, writing, or reading she enjoys spending time with family and friends and embracing the weirdness and wonder that is the Pacific Northwest. K.A. loves to cook and is often found tinkering in the kitchen and trying to feed anyone that walks through her door. She is obsessed with music, so if you find yourself at a metal show in Portland —take a look around— she's the crazy redhead head banging at the front.

Also By K.A. Ware

The DeLuca Family Series

Omertá

Vendetta

Notorious

Bloodline

Fracture

Swamp Bottom Series

Front Porches and Funerals

Voodoo and Vodka

Hook-Ups and Hang-Ups

Blue Lights and Boatmen

Pink Lines and Panic

Divorce and Denial

Warrants and Onesies

Coming Soon

Knights of Mayhem MC Series

Tempt My Trouble

Made in the USA
Middletown, DE
29 October 2018